THE MURDER AT KENDRICK MANOR

JODY DERBY

COMBOBULATE PUBLISHING

CONTENTS

CHAPTER 1

L ily swung the travel case onto her bed, snapped off the price tag, and pulled the zip. Behind her, an emerald dress hung on the back of the door, giving a flash of vibrancy in the otherwise magnolia room. Lily gazed at the dress protected under a clear plastic cover, and with her hands on her hips, she admired the delicate beading as it glistened in the lamplight. She couldn't, strictly, afford it. Not if she ever hoped to save up enough money to move out of the houseshare, but, as she'd won her ticket to Kendrick Manor, she reasoned she deserved a treat. She couldn't be sensible all the time.

It was a Friday in late October and night had started early. Lily peered outside. On the street below, people busied past, some with umbrellas, others not, as the autumn drizzle teased them. She drew the thin curtains on the world and carried on packing, folding the dress in half and placing it in the case on top of a spare pair of jeans and her most comfortable nightwear.

Steve, her housemate, knocked on the door. The friendly one. He liked to pop round after football practice and she liked to pretend to be interested in his sporting achievements. He had a kind soul, and it didn't hurt to listen to him for a few minutes each week. He always tried to convince her to join him and the others at the pub, and she always refused the invitation. She didn't want to seem rude, she just had other priorities.

Steve hovered in the hall. 'Hey, Lils.'

He wore a sweaty sports kit and stripes of mud smeared across his cheek, like some sort of footballing warrior.

'Hi, Steve,' she replied, grateful he'd opted to stay on the other side of the threshold rather than sprinkle mud dust over the impractical cream carpet.

She moved across the room to the battered desk in the alcove, lowered the lid of her laptop and flipped over the ringed notebook at its side. She knew he couldn't see the photos and note cards pinned to the corkboard from where he stood. Steve propped his shoulder against the door frame.

His phone pinged and his attention flicked to it before he asked, 'Where you off to?'

Lily did a pirouette. 'Ah,' she said. 'I'm off to witness a weekend of murder.'

Steve laughed. ''Course you are. So, once again, you're not coming to the pub.'

Lily wasn't going to indulge him, but she couldn't fault him for trying. 'No, Steve.'

'Shameful. Well, at least you've got a good excuse this week. We were beginning to think you don't want to be friends.'

He gave her a wink. One Lily imagined would leave most women's hearts fluttering. Not that she could ever think of him like that, and anyway, she was far too busy for a relationship.

'Well,' he said. 'Just make sure you don't end up being the one to get knocked off.'

'It's fictional.'

'You say that now, but you'd better tell me where it is. That way we can come rescue you if it all goes a bit horror movie.'

He wiggled his fingers in the air as he spoke, and Lily couldn't help but smile at the thought of a bunch of drunken amateur footballers descending on the 1920s scene, on a quest to save her from certain death. But she humoured him and held up the glossy brochure, knowing it would impress, excited to see his reaction.

She'd been impressed herself when it had arrived a few days earlier, crisp and shiny in an A4 envelope, along with a ticket printed on expensive paper. The cover showed the imposing facade of the manor set in lush grounds under a blue sky. He leaned in and reached out to take the brochure for a closer look.

She pulled it back, just out of reach. 'Not with those muddy paws.'

'Oh, fancy.' Steve held up his hands in mock surrender. 'So, just to confirm, you're definitely not coming to the pub?'

'Out.' She swatted at him. 'I'll be back on Sunday and promise to tell you all about my brilliant powers of deduction.'

'Fair enough.' He brushed his hair off his face. 'Okay, have fun. I'd better grab a quick shower. We'll see you when you get back.'

He ambled down the cluttered hallway to the shared bathroom without giving her a second glance.

Lily needed to get going and did a last sweep of the room. She made sure the books that lined the floor were in a straight row, checked she'd locked the window and zipped up the neatly packed case. She slipped the brochure into her bag. It promised her an unforgettable experience. To step back in time, to the golden age of mystery, where anyone could be the victim and everyone was a suspect. Lily couldn't wait.

Lily trundled along the high street beneath street lights that were just a touch too dim to keep away the gloom. Soggy leaves stuck to the wheels of the travel case and moisture clung to her hair. She didn't mind. She dodged the early evening commuters, heads down, making their way home. The shops were still open, their wares illuminated behind glazed frontages that attempted to entice.

Clusters of colleagues and friends huddled under the awning of a pub, spilling out beyond the wooden planters intended to mark the boundary. She skirted around them and through a nicotine cloud. At the busy road, a black cab slowed to let her cross. She raised her palm in thanks, but didn't raise her head. The grey block of Clapham North tube station balanced on the intersection between two streets, sucking in the evening's travellers. She moved with them, swerved a group of tourists gathered at the entrance and tapped through the barriers, absorbed by the crowd.

Lily paused at the top of the wide stairs to the platform. A harassed father knocked her shoulder as he bumped a pushchair laden with shopping bags, but missing a child, down each step. People rushed past, keen to catch the train pulling up at the station. No one offered to help. People seldom did, preferring not to get involved. It wasn't polite, and it wasn't Lily's style. She darted in front of him and lifted the front of the pram to assist, bumping her case along beside her. At the bottom, she let go and walked away while a fiery mother dropped a wriggling toddler into the seat. A brief and animated exchange ensued between them in a language Lily recognised but didn't understand. Neither of them acknowledged her. It didn't matter.

As Lily left them behind, moving along the slabs, the platform filled. Regular commuters pushed past those who weren't familiar with the rules of this subterranean world. They claimed their preferred places where the doors would open. For once, Lily didn't join the rush. She found a space next to the map that imparted its wisdom to a cluster of tourists, who traced their journeys along the coloured lines beneath the Perspex.

Lily peeked up at the display where digital orange numbers confirmed her wait would be short. To her side, a woman in a tailored woollen coat and trainers read the evening paper. Her laptop poked out of an oversized designer bag.

A gang of teenagers in black school uniforms gathered at the far end of the platform. Their ties were loose and their backpacks dumped in a careless pile on the floor. They harboured no concerns about pick-pockets. Their phones were the only thing of value to them and each held on to their device as they alternated between real-life conversations and those online.

Lily observed her fellow travellers until electricity pumped through the tracks. The train emerged from the tunnel, accompanied by the crackled instructions from the guard over the tannoy, requesting that passengers be permitted to 'get off the train first'. As Lily shuffled forwards, a tall man in a leather jacket sauntered past. A teenager jerked his chin at him in some sort of urban salute. One of their teachers, perhaps.

A dance began. One where those who wished to leave the carriage manoeuvred around those who wished to stay. Most people ignored the tannoy's plea, and the departers were forced to squeeze through a small channel left by the boarding hordes. Lily, however, waited patiently and stepped on board just as the doors slid closed behind her. She spotted an unclaimed seat in the carriage's body and made her way towards it. She lifted her case over feet and concentrated on not treading on any toes. A child cried in the background. The micro-climate inside the carriage was warm and damp. Wet umbrellas, propped against people's legs, dripped on the floor. Jackets were unzipped as the humidity made the wearers crave a little air. Passengers concentrated on smartphones or newspapers.

The man from the platform claimed the seat opposite her. After shrugging out of the leather jacket, he folded it over his holdall and tucked both behind his long legs. He wore a black T-shirt that revealed a pattern of intricate tattoos decorating his arms. He caught her watching him. Heat flushed around Lily's neck and she loosened her scarf, attempting to pretend it was a complete coincidence she'd been looking in his direction. She averted her gaze, focusing instead on the shoes of the woman next to him before he could spot her staring again. He rubbed his hand across his short dark hair, and with the deliberate focus of someone intent on avoiding all human interaction, he reached down to the holdall where he pulled out a glossy brochure printed on expensive paper. A brochure of Kendrick Manor.

Chapter 2

Max gripped the brochure on his lap and concentrated on his breathing. In. Out. Just like the counsellor advised. In through the nose, out through the mouth. His hands shook. The edges of his vision blurred in a red haze. In. Out. The woman across from him kept staring, like she knew he was about to descend into a full-blown panic attack. In. Out.

He'd meant to leave for Kendrick Manor hours ago, but each time he'd thought he was ready, he'd found some other supposedly vital task he felt compelled to complete before he left. So, by the time he had locked up the flat, it was dark outside, and he got caught in rush hour. Bad combination. He hated being late, and since he'd lost Theo, he couldn't handle crowds. God, he missed him. So much for a straightforward journey. On the plus side, at least the kids from the platform had bundled into a different carriage. The last thing he needed was anyone at the youth centre hearing about him fainting on the train. Talk about destroy his credibility.

The woman was still staring. Great. Just as long as she didn't want to make conversation. She didn't look like one of the overfamiliar travellers you sometimes get on the Tube, quite the opposite. Pretty, in an understated way that implied she probably didn't realise the effect she had. He saw the same lack of confidence in the girls at the centre all the time, and he tried to reinforce that it was just as important to develop their minds as their make-up skills. Sometimes he got through. Not as often as he'd like, but often enough to make the effort worthwhile.

Max fanned himself with the brochure and tried to pretend he hadn't noticed the woman. The heavy thud of dance music escaped from the earbuds of the man next to him. The train rocked. Max breathed.

'Excuse me.' She leaned forwards.

Brilliant. Now she'd decided to talk to him as well.

'I'm sorry to disturb you. I think we might be going to the same place.'

She held up a glossy brochure of her own. Proof she was telling the truth. Apart from being less dog-eared, it was the same as his.

She carried on. 'I'm not sure we're allowed to meet before the event. They might think it's cheating.'

The train pulled up at Monument station and the doors slid open, letting in a cool breeze. Not as restorative as fresh air, but enough. Max had made it through the worst part of the journey, and now it appeared he'd gained a companion.

'I reckon we'll get away with it.' He stood. 'I think we need to change here.'

'We do.' She lifted her case. 'I'm Lily, by the way.'

They got off the train together, moving with the swarm.

'Max,' he said.

They bustled through the twisting maze of tunnels, past a busker playing guitar, and out onto the platform of the Docklands Light Railway. The damp evening air cooled Max's skin, and he put his jacket back on.

They sat side by side at the front of the driverless train as it snaked between tall blocks of flats, the pyramid of Canary Wharf lit up in the distance.

'Have you done much prep for the weekend?' Max asked.

'A bit,' she said. 'I've been reading lots of mystery books and bingeing all the old shows on TV, but I sort of do that normally. How about you?'

'Same.'

That wasn't strictly true. Max did like mystery. He'd just had more important things on his mind recently.

Lily stared out of the window. Not that there was much to see at this time of night. 'I wonder what the others will be like.'

'At least we get to play ourselves,' Max said. 'I'm not sure pretending to be a duke, eccentric entrepreneur, or something similar would have been quite up my street.'

Lily chuckled. 'I know what you mean. I've memorised my clues, but what you see is what you get and you needn't think I'm sharing.' Her tone teased, and she wagged her finger at him.

He couldn't remember the last time he'd met anyone so easy to enjoy a joke with.

'Competitive much?'

'Actually, no. Not really.' Her shoulders dropped, suddenly serious, and he worried he'd hit a nerve. 'I just find it fascinating how they put these things together.'

'Suppose.'

She perceived the pause. 'Then why are you going?' Her expression revealed an innocent curiosity.

Might as well tell her the truth.

'Someone donated the ticket to the youth centre I work at. Apparently, the owners of the manor are considering community options and might want to offer events for the kids. I'm just checking it out to make sure it's appropriate.' That was enough. He didn't need to say any more. 'How 'bout you?'

She ignored his question. 'So that's how you knew the teenagers at the station.'

'Yup.'

She was observant. He'd have to watch out for that.

She carried on. 'I won my ticket.' Her face shone with delight, while her voice remained humble. 'I wrote a story, and it won a competition.'

'Nice,' he said, impressed. The train pulled up at the station. 'I think this is us. Can't believe I didn't bring a brolly. The rain's got worse.'

A firework scattered golden light across the sky as it exploded above them. The air smelled of sulphur.

'We could try to get a cab,' Max said. 'I don't like our chances, though. It's not that far, but I think it's mostly uphill.'

'Yeah, we might be lucky.'

They wandered across to the taxi rank to find a long queue of people and a distinct lack of vehicles.

'Okay,' he said. 'We've got two choices. We can either wait in the rain, or walk in the rain.'

Lily checked her phone. 'Wonderful. Off we go, then. It's this way.' She pointed up the street and pulled her case behind her as she marched off. Max threw his holdall over his shoulder and followed. No going back now.

CHAPTER 3

J amie McKensey fastened his tweed jacket. When he'd bought the suit, he'd thought it would itch, but got it anyway because it made him look the part. He'd been pleasantly surprised with how comfortable it turned out to be. Appearances were so important. He reached down, and used a cloth to finish polishing the black Oxfords he'd wear when the guests arrived, but for now, he accessorised his outfit with a pair of his favourite brand of canvas trainers. He admired the effect in the full-length mirror propped in the corner of the cramped attic room, amazed by what one could achieve with a little imagination, effort, and some careful planning.

The Georgian manor came with the customary collection of period features: alcoves, ironwork, marble, and a series of narrow passages and staircases weaving through the walls, hidden behind elaborate wooden panels. Jamie marvelled that when the house had been at its prime, whole lives were lived in these secret spaces, unknown and uninteresting to the owners of the property.

He left his room and halted on a patch of hallway with four doors leading off. Jamie rapped a rhythm on one of them and pulled it open without waiting for a reply. His friend and business partner, Elliot Windsor, sat in a leather armchair, hunched over a laptop balanced on his knees. A second armchair nestled under the eaves, with a low coffee table in between. Elliot chewed his bottom lip as he switched his attention between a laptop and four flat-screens mounted on the opposite wall. Jamie dropped into the empty chair and tapped the armrest.

Elliot ignored him while he finished whatever he was doing. Jamie waited until he was ready, impressed once more with his patience.

Elliot pushed his glasses up his nose. 'Done.'

Like Jamie, Elliot wore period clothes, but he'd opted for a traditional morning, rather than tweed, suit. Freshly pressed and crisp against his pale skin, with a grey double-breasted waistcoat underneath. The silver chain from a pocket watch looped along his side, and a silk bowtie adorned his neck. He gave the impression of being every bit the historic city gentleman until he spoke, and his modern Estuary accent gave him away.

They'd met as children. At primary school, when Jamie joined halfway through a term. The stern teacher had marched him to the front of a hostile classroom. While he'd towered above her, he couldn't remember ever feeling so small, as he'd undergone judgement from a room of children with established friendships and no vacancies for him. He'd slumped next to a boy with heavy glasses, who'd blinked a welcome that began their friendship.

But they weren't children anymore. Now Elliot opted for modern square frames and even though he'd cropped his once wavy dark hair, you could still make out flecks of silver highlights. They weren't old, they insisted, just a little more established than they'd been before.

'You ready?' Elliot said.

'As I'll ever be.' Jamie stretched his legs in front of him and crossed them at the ankles.

On the screen, a rotation of images displayed the rooms of the house, each decorated with details designed to enhance the mystery of the weekend. Deep maroons, mahogany and brass. When the guests arrived, he and Elliot would transport them back into the past, to the golden era of crime. They'd positioned clues in communal areas and hidden cameras to observe their discoveries.

Eight guests were about to descend on Kendrick Manor. Some had won their place, others had received an invitation as a gift of sorts, but each had been selected with care for their interest in mystery and their unique skills. Like the classic novels, the guests were distinctive in every other way. There was the bookworm, the retired detective, and the man who cared full-time for his elderly mother. The perfect archetypes for murder mystery attendees.

Jamie leaned forwards to inspect the image of the drawing room where so much of the weekend's action was scheduled to take place. Two Chesterfield sofas lined an antique rug, accompanied by four wingback chairs in the same chestnut leather. The imposing marble mantelpiece held a genuine vintage carriage clock and, above it, hung a framed oil painting. Beneath grand cornicing, deep olive wallpaper. Jamie had dedicated more time to designing this room than any other and considered it his own masterpiece.

'All set downstairs,' he said. 'Showtime.'

'All done here too. Pretty sure you forgot something, though.' Elliot gave a mocking scowl as he pointed to the offending footwear.

Jamie crossed his heart, gave a Scout's salute, and promised to change before the guests arrived. Elliot closed the laptop and slipped it onto the coffee table. He pushed Jamie out of the attic door with a brotherly shove.

The slim staircase that transported them from the old servants' quarters down into the main house was like a portal through time. Upstairs, they'd installed the modern technology that would help them monitor and guide the weekend. They'd kept the decoration minimal and functional. Downstairs, the wide landing was opulent. Plush carpet and walnut furniture created the impression that this was a home for the wealthy. Each bedroom door adorned with a brass plaque indicating its theme. They separated. Checked each room one last time, making sure the silver trays of tea- and coffee-making facilities were stocked, the beds were smoothed and that each possessed the correct envelope with the guests' instructions.

They reconvened on the mezzanine by the grand staircase sweeping through the middle of the building. Nearly time. The guests would start arriving any minute.

'Shoes.' Elliot pointed as he gave his command.

'Yes, sir!' Jamie bounded up the stairs two at a time, spun round at the top and gave another mock salute before he disappeared behind the wooden panel leading to the attic.

Jamie settled in the battered armchair and followed Elliot on the screen, shuffling around the drawing room. He rearranged a vase of pink carnations that were already perfectly presentable in the centre of the table. He kept glancing at the hidden cameras. Jamie narrowed his eyes. He'd need to make sure he didn't do that once the guests arrived. The empty rooms rotated on the screen's carousel. Not long till they'd be filled with murder and suspicion. Jamie folded his arms. This was it. Everything they'd worked for.

CHAPTER 4

T he wheels of Lily's case bounced along cobbles that must have been practical once upon a time, but certainly no longer were.

'I can carry that for you,' Max said.

'It's fine.' There was no way her feminist pride would allow that.

He didn't push the point. They made their way along the twisting paths of Greenwich, where Victorian terraces built for the working-classes were now prime real estate.

Although they were technically still in London, conservation orders protected the area from the over-development of other parts of the capital, and Lily loved it there. Outside the town centre, the streets widened, ancient trees lining the pavements, their remaining leaves turning orange. They walked past tall houses where affluent families lived in large homes, still intact and not converted into flats or houseshares, like where she lived. Designer decor showcased behind windows yet to be covered by curtains for the night. Expensive cars waited in private parking bays and secret gardens hid behind iron gates.

Max whistled. 'How the other half live. To think what we could do with the price of one of those cars.'

'I know what you mean.' Lily looked across at the car in question. 'That's probably worth more than I earn in a year.'

Max adjusted his holdall. 'And what do you do?'

'I work for an IT company. Not that I'm a techie or anything, I'm in marketing.'

Max pulled the same face as most people did when she told them what she did. Like they didn't understand what she'd said, but didn't want to offend her. To his credit, he recovered quickly.

'More importantly, do you enjoy it?'

'Well, it's not my dream job, if that's what you mean, but the people are nice…'

'And you wrote a story to win your invitation to the manor. That's brilliant. Are you writing anything else?'

They reached a pedestrian crossing and waited for the lights to change.

'That's the dream.' Lily shifted the umbrella. 'I'd love to write a book one day and I'm really hoping this weekend will help me find the inspiration.'

'You can do anything you set your mind to, with enough hard work.'

Not sure if he was teasing her or was sincere, she slowed. 'And you sound like you're giving a pep talk to one of your teenagers.'

'Sorry, force of habit.'

Lily found him easy to talk to, and could see why the young people he worked with would feel comfortable with him. She'd better be careful not to let any of her clues slip once they arrived at the manor. She suspected he'd be one of those people able to get others to open up, with no effort at all, and while she wasn't all that fussed about winning, she wanted to respect the rules of the game and enjoy the experience.

They made their way up the hill and towards the heath. Despite the rain, it was warmer than Lily expected at this time of year, and the added exertion of pulling the case was making her clammy. She yanked the scarf from her neck, folded it in half, and tied it to the strap of her bag. Street dirt stuck to the ends of her shoes. Her arm ached from pulling the case, and she found coordinating the umbrella difficult.

'We're nearly there,' Max reassured her, as if reading her thoughts. 'Then we can dry off and get a hot drink.'

'About time.' She'd not meant to snap at him. 'Sorry. I'm just annoyed at myself for not planning the journey better. I'd wanted to arrive ready to make a good impression.'

'It'll be fine,' he said. 'We'll get all dressed up in our old-fashioned costumes and forget all about our wet jeans.'

'Right again.' Lily remembered her emerald dress and how excited she was to wear it, and anyway, a short walk in the rain never did anyone any harm.

Kendrick Manor loomed up ahead. A detached property nestled in one corner of the heath. The other buildings in the vicinity kept a respectful distance, and the manor maintained its privacy behind grand iron railings. A building this grand must have stories to tell and Lily was determined to find out more than the brief details hinted at in the invitation. She'd brought a new notebook with her and intended to fill its pages with research and ideas.

Lily sighed. 'Finally.'

They stepped through the open gate and walked side by side down the driveway. Their feet crunched on the gravel as they followed a row of lights guiding their way towards a two-storey, red brick structure with deep bay windows on the ground floor. Lily tried not to rush. They both stopped making small talk, intuition instructing them to enjoy and absorb their first impressions in silence. They reached the black wooden front door and sheltered under the awning. Lily fumbled with her umbrella until she made it collapse. Max lowered his holdall and pressed the round doorbell.

'Here we go.'

Lily fidgeted, slipped her hands into her pockets. Took them out again and rubbed them together. If Max realised, he didn't say anything.

When the door swung back, warmth and light spilled out, revealing a man in a morning suit. He wore glasses, and the chain from a pocket watch looped along one side of his jacket.

'Welcome to Kendrick Manor,' he said. His voice was as aristocratic as his appearance. 'Won't you please come in out of the rain?' He gave a sweep of his hand and took a slight step back, allowing them to enter.

The door slammed shut behind them.

CHAPTER 5

F inally, the guests were arriving. Jamie leaned forwards in the attic chair, wanting to be closer to the action. He'd stay behind the scenes for a while longer, getting more of an idea about their chosen attendees. The woman, Lily, was petite with light brown hair and a face full of fascination, pretty in an understated way, with just a dash of drowned rat. She dropped her umbrella into the metal stand and twisted her head this way and that, as Elliot showed her and Max through to the drawing room. Max appeared more reserved. Like he didn't want to be caught spying on the house's splendour. An unusual pair. Incongruous in their damp, modern clothes.

They entered the drawing room, and Elliot took up position beside a mahogany desk. He checked his pocket watch. It didn't work, but the guests wouldn't know that. Jamie couldn't resist when he'd found it in an antique shop in Brighton. Elliot had been delighted. It's always the little things. He slipped the watch back into his pocket and settled his palms on the edge of the table next to a large leather-bound book waiting open with blank pages. An art deco desk lamp cast a warm light over the table. Lily and Max waited to be addressed. Lily gripped the handle of her travel case. When Elliot spoke, he'd use the clipped, received pronunciation he and Jamie had spent long hours practising. Just the right side of aristocratic, without being too intimidating. Jamie tented his fingers and waited for the words. Elliot could do this. Jamie held his breath.

'Welcome to Kendrick Manor.' He got the intonation spot on. 'My name is Elliot Windsor, and I will be your host for the weekend.' He offered his hand to Lily, and she released the case she'd been gripping on to like a life preserver.

'Lily Jones.' She reached forwards.

Elliot held her hand for just a fraction longer than necessary. Jamie tensed – it was not part of the plan – but his friend recovered quickly. He released her and switched his attention to Max, who made his own introduction in a deep, confident voice.

'Isaac Maxwell,' he said. 'Everyone calls me Max.'

Elliot cast his eyes up and down the rain-soaked pair, appraising them in the way an aristocrat might, as though he were considering their worth. They'd practised that too. He was doing well. Jamie shifted in his chair.

'You are both most welcome.' Elliot stepped behind the desk. 'If I could ask you to take a moment and sign the guest book. Then I'll show you up to your rooms. I'm sure you're keen to dry off and relax after your journey. Awful weather. I hope it doesn't interfere with your enjoyment of the weekend.' He passed an antique fountain pen to Lily.

She accepted and signed her name in a shaking cursive. 'Look at this.' She held up her trembling hand. 'I'm showing my nerves already.'

'Must be a guilty conscience.' Max took the pen and signed his own name.

Lily moved her hand to her chest. 'The cheek.'

Somehow, they'd already developed a friendship of sorts, if the banter was anything to go by. It would be interesting to see how that played out.

Elliot picked up on it, too. 'Excuse my asking,' he said, 'but have you two met before?' He balanced on the front edge of the desk. He kept his tone serious, not too chatty. Another thing they'd practised.

Max shrugged. 'No, we just happened to get the same train here. Complete coincidence.'

'I hope that's okay,' Lily said as she studied the floor. 'You won't consider it an unfair advantage or anything.'

'Of course, it's absolutely fine,' Elliot said. 'Your role is to watch for the clues, after all. That you managed to deduce your mutual destination before the game's begun is marvellous. Those skills will be even more important now you're here.'

Elliot coped with the curve ball well. It impressed Jamie. He couldn't have handled it better himself.

Elliot laced his fingers together and went back to the script. 'We know a crime will be committed and it will be your task to unveil both the culprit and the motive.'

He reassured them they were perfectly safe. The detailed game would be challenging, but not impossible.

'We've selected you to join us because of your unique abilities. We intend to open to the public later this year and you're doing us a great service by sharing your expertise. There are a few rules, as you'd expect. First, we ask that you respect our no-technology policy. There's a safe in each of the rooms for you to lock your electronic devices away.'

Lily wrinkled her nose.

Elliot pushed on, as if the reassurance were part of what he'd intended to say all along. 'The manor is not a prison. You will select the code yourself and will have access to your belongings whenever you wish. You are completely free to leave whenever you so choose. But, I must make it clear, if you do decide to leave before the mystery is complete, you won't be readmitted, as it would simply spoil things for the others.'

He delivered the speech in the same elegant voice, smooth, and just the right side of mysterious. Even from the attic, Jamie could see how his eyes sparkled with the pleasure of it all. Elliot rose with a jump, pulled open a drawer and collected two brass keys.

He strode out of the drawing room and called back over his shoulder. 'This way, please.'

Lily and Max followed as they'd been asked to. Past the portraits lining the stairs and on to the mezzanine, where Elliot halted and inserted the first key into a varnished wooden door with a single adornment: a bronze plaque naming the room 'Manderley'.

'For you.' He gave Lily a half smile as he opened the door a crack. 'Max, if you'd like to follow me.'

He left Lily to get settled in and carried on to what would be Max's room without so much as a sideways glance at the cameras. Elliot had surpassed Jamie's expectations. So far, so good.

CHAPTER 6

D ebbie shut down her computer. From behind the clear partition separating her office from the main floor, she could observe, but thankfully not hear, the buzz of Friday night revelry. Another end to yet another busy week, and while some workers were focusing, bashing out their last important tasks, others were already packing bags ready for an after-work drink. Debbie preferred to work late, regardless of what day of the week it was. However, this evening, this weekend, she'd made different plans.

Milly, her PA, popped her head around the glass door. A young woman with the social media poise of a reality TV star, bronzed skin and long false eyelashes. She was also one of the most capable and diligent staff Debbie had ever worked with. She might not be what you'd expect, but people so often judged a book by its cover, only to find out later they were wrong.

'I just wanted to check you've everything you need before I make a move?'

Milly would be part of the pub crowd, and later move on to meet friends and dance the night away. Debbie had never understood the appeal of crushing into a nightclub, but then, as she was well aware, she was no longer their desired demographic, thank heaven. She reached into her leather satchel for her purse and pulled out a few crisp notes.

'Get the troops a round on me.' She waved the notes at Milly. Drinks on the boss always went down well, and she'd expense it later.

'Thanks.' Milly gave her a sparkling Hollywood smile. 'I've confirmed the taxi from yours to the manor and I've let Mr Windsor know about your allergy. He's assured me there'll be no soy products used in the kitchen.'

'Perfect.' Debbie stood and took her cashmere coat from the stand. 'I've high hopes for this weekend. There's been a lot of change here over the past few months and a team-building activity is just what people need. If this trial run goes well, I intend to book something in for the top performers before Christmas.'

Debbie made the tough decisions, and she'd pushed through a number of challenging initiatives since she'd been head-hunted six months ago. Restructuring was a messy but necessary task, and now it was done it was time to reinforce the commitment of the remaining staff. She was the leading sales director in the industry and her results spoke for themselves, yet it had still taken some convincing to get the board to agree.

She'd tasked Milly with researching motivational activities and reviewed a wide variety of options, from mountain climbing, paint-balling, and white-water rafting, through to life drawing, quilt making, and butchery. And then she'd received a brochure for a murder mystery weekend at an old Georgian property just on the outskirts of the city. Not too active, nothing that would give the health-and-safety people palpitations and nothing that risked offending people's personal beliefs.

'I really hope it goes well.' Milly smoothed the sides of her pencil skirt. 'I quite fancy myself as a detective and getting all dressed up in fancy vintage clothes. Sounds fun.'

Debbie buttoned her coat. 'Yes, well, it won't all be fun and games, and I've got no desire to get all worked up to uncover a pretend crime.'

Milly laughed. 'Have you met you? No offence, but you're one of the most competitive people I've ever met. I'll be amazed if you don't win.'

'You make a valid point,' Debbie conceded, fastening the satchel. She wouldn't let that kind of comment slide from any of the rest of the staff, but from Milly, she considered it a compliment. 'We'll see. I still need to finish up that presentation for Monday, so I doubt I'll be able to give it my full attention. Anyway, enjoy your evening, and I'll report back with my evaluation next week.'

'Sounds like a plan.' Milly backed away and joined the others congregating in the office kitchen, enjoying a pre-pub glass of wine.

Debbie shut the door to her corner office, and in the atrium, she pressed the chrome button for the lift. On the ground floor, she wished the receptionist, whose name she didn't know, a good weekend and marched out into the October evening drizzle. On the bustling city streets, people rushed around doing whatever it was people do on Friday nights. She reached the station and checked her train time on the notice board, pleased it was on schedule, which was becoming a rarity. She navigated the crowds, swerved a yellow sign warning her of the slippery floor and then around a couple who halted, for no apparent reason, directly in front of her. No wonder people detested rush hour.

She spotted her train pulling in, tapped through the barrier and marched to the end of the platform, where she waited at the precise place where the doors would open. The people heading into the city were mainly young, on their way out for the evening. Dressed inappropriately for the weather and drinking cheap alcohol from cans. A few older travellers glared, not bothering to hide their disapproval from the youngsters. They must be the theatre set, she assumed.

Debbie brushed an empty crisp packet to the floor and sat in her preferred seat at the back of a carriage. As the train pulled away, the lights of the city faded behind her. She pulled out her laptop and carried on with the client presentation for Monday. It might be her weekend off, but she still had plenty of work to do.

The train crawled through the suburbs, late now, and with no explanation provided. As they finally pulled into the station, Debbie put her laptop away and waited by the door, her finger poised over the button, ready to release herself and the others as soon as the light changed. She hurried through the rain, frustrated at the delay.

Her home would be considered modest compared to those of her peers, but it suited her needs, and even though she could have afforded to, she'd resisted up-sizing. She'd bought the property almost five years ago, and although it was a bit of a commute, she didn't mind the journey, preferring to be on the early train in, and the late train home. It meant she could take advantage of the quiet as she joined the tradespeople huddled in their seats, enjoying a few minutes of precious sleep, the people with suitcases en route to catch dawn flights, and a handful of other regulars like her, tapping away on their laptops. She treasured being able to gather her thoughts before the noise of the day.

Debbie unlocked her front door and dropped her keys into a ceramic dish. She slipped off her heels and reached inside her bag to find an antacid. Lateness irked her, and she hated breaking routine, but weakness was not a quality to be admired and it was not a quality she intended to display. Milly might be right. The weekend could be fun. She couldn't remember when she'd last experienced any of that. There was so little time for such things. She was used to working hard and being busy. It gave her purpose. There was something unsettling about the unplanned. Still, she'd have her laptop, and she expected there'd be plenty of time to carry on with her presentation. She'd be able to get up before the others to check her emails, make sure strategic priorities were on track, and she might even squeeze in some reading.

A designer cabin case lay open on the floor in one of her spare rooms. She added a bag of cosmetics and carried it down to the hallway, where she sat on the old church pew her interior designer had convinced her added character. He'd been right. Debbie had given him a generous bonus. Her phone pinged with a text from the taxi driver, letting her know it was waiting outside for her.

The automatic lights went off as she locked up and climbed into the back seat. She gave the address, and for once allowed herself to relax and ponder the next few days, grateful the driver didn't feel the need to make small talk. They twisted through the Friday night traffic, made worse because of the rain. The driver was competent and made good time. Before long, the car slowed, passing through an iron gate. They crunched along the gravel driveway. Ground lights showed them the way to the stately manor. Quite spectacular, even in the dark. The brochure hadn't done it justice. Debbie took another antacid from her bag.

CHAPTER 7

L ily dropped her damp coat over the handle of her case. She slipped off her loafers, not wanting to contaminate the beauty of the room with the debris of her journey. As she took small, cautious steps around the room, her socks sank into the soft carpet. She traced the edge of the pure white bedspread and felt the cotton bumps from the delicate pink embroidery along the edge. A round table nestled by the window, holding a cut-glass tray, a small kettle and a vintage china teacup and saucer, along with a matching teapot. She slid out a small, velvet-lined drawer that held a selection of individual tea and coffee sachets waiting in neat rows to be brewed. A warm drink was just what she needed. She flicked on the kettle and added a bag of Earl Grey to the pot.

Lily pulled her phone from her pocket and allowed herself to take a single photo of the room. Then, as per Elliot's instructions, she knelt down to find the safe at the bottom of the wardrobe. Apart from the kettle, it was the only modern item she'd seen since she'd arrived. She chose a PIN for the safe, her sister's birthday, and held the door closed, waiting for the lock to engage.

She settled into the room, hung the dress in the wardrobe, and slid her case under the bed. A copper candleholder stood empty on the nightstand. Lily searched for candles, but couldn't find any. A dressing table covered with a lace cloth rested by the window. They'd even provided a notepad and pen. The room smelled faintly of lavender.

Cradling the cup, she searched the darkness outside the window. She couldn't tell if it had stopped raining. Clouds hid the stars and there was no streetlight or traffic noise like she was used to. Lily drank her tea and considered the journey. What a strange coincidence bumping into Max like that. Him sitting opposite her and pulling out the brochure. He wasn't exactly what you'd expect a murder mystery fan to resemble. But then, she supposed she didn't fit the stereotype either. He seemed nice enough from the little she'd learned so far, and she looked forward to finding out what the other guests would be like.

Then there was their host, Elliot Windsor. What a character. Lily was pretty sure his accent must be fake. Nobody spoke in received pronunciation anymore unless they were acting. He sounded like he belonged on an archived recording from the BBC. She did, however, sense his charm and energy were genuine. His comfort in the starched morning suit was evident, and she couldn't imagine him in a modern setting. He kept checking his pocket watch, even though clocks scattered through the house united to chime the hour; it implied he was on a schedule, and she always appreciated efficient organisation.

A white envelope rested on the end of the bed. Lily settled the cup on the waiting saucer and slipped her finger under the envelope's flap to break the wax seal. She winced as the sharp edge sliced her skin; she sucked her finger, annoyed at her clumsiness. The wicker armchair creaked as she lowered herself into it. She took another sip of tea and soon became absorbed in the typewritten story, the words surrounded by a decorative mint border. She forgot her surroundings as she read the message left just for her. The story of the house, the origin of the idea and some more instructions about how she could stay in character during the weekend. She took her time and searched for clues within the words.

The remarkable house you are staying in was once considered relatively humble. Built in the early 1800s, it was the home to an average family, in a time when average meant grandeur; at least when compared to modern expectations. The family required their servants to be invisible, hence the secret doors and hidden staircases that ensured they were always available but kept firmly in their place.

The house was full of life. The nanny kept busy in the nursery as more children arrived, the cook catering for the growing unit and their friends, and the butler, stoic, meticulous, yet easy to overlook.

As they are wont to do, the building developed over the years; adapted to the fashions of the day, weathered wars, and welcomed the guests of prosperity. It stood solid, while its generations grew up and moved away. Until there was only one. A last inhabitant, without next of kin. A solitary occupant who adapted a single room to accommodate their ageing needs. When they passed from this world, they left the house vacant. The grandeur slipped away, replaced by cobwebs and darkness, and like a fairy-tale, it waited to be brought back to life.

Your hosts for the weekend are Elliot Windsor, who you will have already met, and Jamie McKensey. Your arrival here marks the culmination of an extensive plan and complete dedication to creating an unforgettable mystery experience. This weekend, we invite you to investigate the crime that will soon be committed. Eight of you will take part. The question is, which of you will leave alive?

CHAPTER 8

Max dropped the holdall, instantly immersed in the room Elliot had allocated him. He was an eccentric man, but then Max liked the unusual. Maybe this weekend was just what he needed after all. A few days without the community constantly asking him if he was okay. A few days just being Max, and not Max, who was grieving. Not that he didn't appreciate how much they cared.

He needed to get ready for this drinks reception and wanted to get out of his wet clothes; instead, he procrastinated by exploring the room. Pretty spectacular by anyone's standards, a re-imagining of an opulent carriage on the *Orient Express*, complete with curved ceilings and walls of polished wooden panels inlaid with intricate patterns. A large bed nestled against the wall, giving the illusion it could fold away during the day. Max checked. It didn't fold. An art deco lamp on a long desk cast green light over the room. A leather writing square held a thick pad of lined paper, and a heavy fountain pen waited for travellers who wished to document their adventures at the end of a busy day of sightseeing. Max examined each new thing as if he were in a museum, appreciating the care and attention given to each detail.

He bent to unzip the holdall. Unpacking wouldn't take long. He'd travelled light through necessity rather than intent, not sure what he needed and not having too wide a wardrobe to choose from in the first place. There was one exception. The invite specified black tie for dinner, in the style of the 1920s. As someone who spent most of his time either in the youth centre with the kids or in the artist's studio, he had a disproportionate need for a suit. There always seemed to be some sort of charity event or gala being arranged.

He lifted out his spare jeans and two T-shirts and put them in the deep middle drawer of the tallboy. Swallowing hard, he unrolled the dinner suit and shirt he'd hoped to prevent creasing. He remembered Theo showing him that trick the first time they'd gone away to an art exhibition. Max learned something from that old man each and every day, no matter how small. He'd always encouraged him not to dwell on things that were in the past, but without him, it was hard. God, he missed him.

An envelope rested on the edge of the bed. Max took his time and read the details typed on heavy paper. As he did, it dawned on him that he was getting into the experience far more than he'd expected to. Before he'd arrived, he hadn't processed that it was basically a competition. He'd just thought he was honouring his obligations by attending. But now, he found, to his surprise, he'd quite like to win. He could imagine Theo laughing at him from his favourite armchair in the corner of the youth centre. A 'told you so' expression on his face.

Suitably reminded of the no-technology rule and food schedule, Max refolded the paper into three, overlapping the ends and reminding the pages of their creases. He put it on the desk by the window and pulled the metal chain to raise the roller-blind and uncover the night. His room looked over the drive he and Lily had just walked up. The light from the entrance stretched a short distance from the house. After that, it was as if the world no longer existed, and they were alone in this make-believe manor. The rush and crowds of the city were far away, and the peace should be healing. He wasn't ready to think about what would happen to him when he got back. Whether he'd sell the flat or stay in it. For now, he could leave his worries out there in the darkness for just a few days.

The shower in the compact en suite ran just the right side of too hot, as Max let the water spill down his back and over his tattooed skin. He'd selected each piece to represent a part of his life, honouring good times and bad. He already knew which design he'd add in remembrance of his friend, and had drawn the template.

Refreshed, he stepped out onto the soft white bathmat and wrapped himself in the towelling robe. He wiped his hand across the mirror to remove the steam and studied the reflection. His old friend had given him confidence, opportunity, and somewhere safe to stay. Theo would have loved the idea of this weekend giving Max an opportunity to heal. Chance had intervened, causing the woman on the train to speak to him at the exact moment he'd been building up to a full-blown panic attack. What an intervention. Lily, she'd said her name was. He'd chosen lilies for Theo's funeral. He might not mention that.

She'd have her own story anyway, her own demons. Most people did. First impressions, though, he liked her. Kind, friendly, a bit on the quirky funny side, nothing not to like, and it made a change from talking to surly teenagers and stressed-out social workers. He pulled on his white dress shirt, inserted silver cufflinks and secured the backs. This weekend would be the divide between the old and the new. He'd release his hold on his grief and move on. He grabbed his pills from the bag and swallowed two without water. Yes. He could do this.

CHAPTER 9

J amie watched the screens in the darkened attic while rain tapped on the window behind him. The remaining guests converged on Kendrick Manor. His view updated as the motion sensors picked up action in the house and grounds. He uncrossed his ankles, but although impatient to be part of the action, he stayed put, stayed hidden. The plan stated he should, and he intended to be meticulous in each detail, sticking to the plan, no matter how frustrated he got. At least he could keep tabs on what was happening from the cameras and microphones hidden around the house in light fitments, picture frames, and even plant pots.

Elliot had improvised effectively when Lily and Max arrived together for some unknown reason. He deposited them in their respective rooms without any drama. Jamie expected and wanted the guests to form alliances as the weekend proceeded, just not beforehand. That wasn't part of the plan and would need careful monitoring. At least they'd reacted to the house as he'd hoped. Full of fascination, and after all those months of work, labouring to transform the manor had been worth it. To his credit, Elliot did well too, practice eventually perfecting that silly accent. Jamie motivated and mocked him in equal measure, careful to keep the teasing to encouragement ratio balanced.

He kicked off his trainers and swapped them with the Elliot-approved and considerably less comfortable Oxfords. When the dining room came up on the screen, Jamie felt drawn to it. He could pop down and do a quick check, just to be sure. He knew he shouldn't, but the guests would all move straight from the entrance to the drawing room and then their rooms, so as long as he kept to the servants' stairs, they wouldn't see him. Decision made. He'd risk a jaunt. He crept downstairs.

The door at the bottom of the servants' staircase opened inwards. Jamie peeked out from behind the tapestry concealing it and, satisfied he had the room to himself, slipped inside. A glorious rosewood table dominated the room, surrounded by slit-backed chairs, their upholstered cushions waiting to welcome the guests. Jamie slid open the drawer of the grand dresser and took out sparkling silver cutlery that he positioned next to the table settings, using a tiny metal ruler to check each piece was in the perfect place. He loved the symmetry almost as much as he loved the grandeur. Behind him hung an oil painting of Hampton Court; his favourite king dominated the scene while in the background a collection of servants awaited their next instruction. The king surveyed proceedings and Jamie liked to think the monarch would approve of the feast planned for that evening.

A simple carriage clock in a wooden case stood on the majestic mantelpiece. A small brass key rested to the side for when it needed to be wound, its soft ticking just audible. Other dressers, side cabinets and low tables hugged the edge of the room, displaying a vast array of period ornaments. In the fireplace, flames crackled behind the iron guard and released the soft scent of citrus into the room, the scented wood a suggestion from Elliot and a nice touch.

The double doors between the drawing and dining rooms opened a crack. Jamie flinched. He stepped back from his work, still holding a fork.

Elliot pushed his glasses up his nose and peered over the table. 'I knew you wouldn't be able to leave this.'

Jamie held up his palms. 'Guilty. I was going mad in the attic, had to do something. And there's no chance they'll bump into me in here. Any more arrivals?'

'Just Kevin,' Elliot said, still in character and speaking in that ridiculous but equally brilliant accent. 'I've left him to get acquainted with his room, but not before he gave me a mile-by-mile summary of all the inadequacies of his journey. Let's see if he has any complaints about the manor. I'll be amazed if we get away unscathed.'

'Or if he gets away unscathed.'

Elliot snorted. 'Arthur and Grace have just sent a message to confirm they're en route and should be with us in about fifteen minutes. So far, so good.'

And it was good. Elliot held the back of a chair. Jamie measured the distance between a plate and a knife, then moved on to the next place setting.

'It'll go to plan.' Jamie nudged the soup spoon a fraction to one side. 'Tell me what the first two are like.' He'd formed his own opinion, but he was interested to hear what Elliot thought.

'First impressions, Lily is quiet, but by the way she scrutinised the decor as she walked around, I'd say she's a contender.'

'Hmm, and Max?'

'Harder to judge. I couldn't tell if he was just a bit standoffish or if he was hiding something. He's quite intimidating to look at and I wouldn't want to cross him. The two of them seemed to be getting along okay. I've no idea how they ended up arriving together.'

Jamie repositioned a fork, and Elliot peered over his glasses at him. 'I think the cutlery might be as straight as it's going to be.'

Jamie whipped his hand away. Elliot had a point. He was fussing. He reached into his inside pocket and retrieved a red plastic lighter to light the candles in the copper holder in the middle of the table. Jamie winked at Elliot. He knew without receiving the reprimand that the appearance of a non-period lighter was most unacceptable. He slipped the offending item back into his pocket. They were ready. The rooms dressed, the clues set, the dinner being prepared. In two short days, it would be over. He snapped back to business.

'Right, I'd better make myself scarce.' He spun round and disappeared behind the tapestry, back up to their control hub and his chair in front of the screens. He stretched his legs out in front of him, crossed them at the ankles, and once again waited for the rest of the guests. Elliot dithered in the hall as the camera pointing at the driveway picked up movement. A black cab pulled up at the entrance.

Arthur and Grace were the only couple invited to the weekend, and while on paper they were elderly, in reality, they were a walking, talking example of period elegance and charm. Arthur climbed out of the taxi first, opened a large purple golf umbrella, and held out his hand for his wife. She placed her gloved fingertips in the offered hand and emerged like a classic film star. She touched her berry lips to Arthur's cheek and together they admired the manor's facade. Despite his advanced years, Arthur carried himself with the air of a man with a lifetime's experience of being listened to. He appeared neat, pressed, and presentable. Grace, impeccable by his side. Arthur paid the driver and Grace hooked her arm through his.

Elliot swung open the front door. 'Good evening and welcome to Kendrick Manor.'

As Elliot ran through his welcome routine, Jamie considered whether they'd taken too extreme a risk by inviting a retired police detective, no matter how charming he and his wife appeared to be. He needed to stop questioning their decisions. Too late to change the plan now.

As Arthur accepted the fountain pen from Elliot and leaned over to sign the guest book, the bell for the front door chimed again. Three heads jerked around at the sound. Jamie flicked the screen back to the entrance, where a slightly bedraggled, middle-aged woman waited for admittance. Carol. She was early. Not ideal. Max and Lily had already met, and now Arthur, Grace, and Carol would too. They'd intended for the guests to meet for the first time at the cocktail reception, where they'd encounter each other in costume and, having spent a little time in their themed rooms, would have an obvious ice breaker to discuss. A detour from the plan this soon in the event could push them off track for the entire weekend. Elliot would need to improvise again. Jamie clenched his fists. He'd only go down to intercept if absolutely necessary.

Elliot collected Carol and showed her into the drawing room. 'Arthur. Grace. Let me introduce you to Carol.' His graciousness implied it was wonderful she'd arrived early, and no inconvenience at all. Good man.

Carol must have made a great deal of effort with her appearance, yet she'd somehow struggled to achieve the desired effect. Her short, bobbed hair wasn't quite straight and had slight kinks in unfortunate places. She patted it incessantly, and wobbled on a pair of kitten heels, still at least a foot shorter than Elliot. Her eyes crinkled around the edges as she smiled at Arthur and Grace and reached across to shake hands.

'Would you mind taking a seat for me, please?' Elliot indicated the sofa. 'I'll show Mr and Mrs Thornton up to their room and be back with you shortly.'

'Aren't you adorable?' Grace swatted the air in front of him. 'Please, call me Grace.'

'It would be my honour.' Elliot picked up their case, and she hooked her arm through Arthur's once more.

'Lead the way,' Arthur said.

Carol did as she'd been asked, without fuss, and settled into an armchair in front of the fire. Elliot allowed little time for more than a passing greeting between the three of them and was soon back on script, welcoming Carol properly, asking her to sign the guest book, and depositing her in her room.

Next came Debbie, the businesswoman whose firm was considering the weekend as some sort of team-building exercise, and finally Harvey, who arrived a little late and disproportionately apologetic. A large man in every sense of the word and full of nerves if the speed he spoke at was any sign.

As Jamie observed from the servants' quarters, eight guests, eight distinct personalities, chosen for their unique skills and abilities, settled into their carefully crafted rooms and the screens emptied of action while they dressed for dinner. While the house was now full of people and possibilities, from the attic, it looked the same as a few hours before. Perfect.

Downstairs, the butler arrived to oversee the evening. A stern man with a serious face that gave no doubt he'd quash any hint of frivolous behaviour. He set about conducting the waiters, a group of youngsters, using their weekend to earn some extra cash.

Jamie imagined the guests would all be reading about the house, their hosts, and absorbing their instructions. Each room contained a safe where they'd lock away their devices. None of history's legendary sleuths were famed for looking up clues on the Internet.

He imagined them changing into their 1920s outfits, ready for the formal reception ahead of dinner at eight. Maybe they'd already be noting down clues. They all knew one of them had been cast as the would-be killer and it was their mission to uncover the criminal. With one exception: the villain themselves, whose goal was to remain hidden. They had until dinner tomorrow to investigate and decide. Tonight, they'd drink cocktails and get to know each other before the crime itself. Then the fun would really begin.

CHAPTER 10

L ily collided with the satin-covered behind of a woman bent double in the
hallway.

'I'm so sorry,' Lily stuttered, not sure whether the tottering woman needed
some help.

The woman twisted to greet her audience while still fiddling with the strap
on her shoe. It didn't help the wobbling.

She gave a self-conscious giggle and straightened herself, still a little unsteady.
'Blasted shoes,' she said. 'I don't know what I was thinking. There's no point to
a kitten heel, anyway. They come with all the same challenges of walking in high
heels, with none of the actual height.'

She held the wall to steady herself, her cheeks flushed pink. A welcoming
woman with just a dash of mischief about her.

'A man must have invented them.' Lily's conspiratorial comment earned a
further giggle from her new acquaintance.

The woman shoved a hand at Lily for her to shake. 'Yes, very good. You're
probably right. I'm Carol, by the way.'

Her bright red nail polish had already chipped at the edges. She wore a purple
satin dress that reached her calves and a long string of pearls tied in front of a
scooped neckline. She patted the back of her wavy blonde hair. Even dressed up,
she radiated a familiar warmth, wholesome and comforting.

Lily took the offered hand. 'Pleased to meet you. I'm Lily. This is all so grand.
I've been impressed so far. My room's amazing, so detailed. What's yours like?'

'Oh, it's just wonderful.' Carol's face broke into a wide smile that revealed a small fleck of lipstick on her front tooth. Lily rubbed her finger along her own teeth, trying to show her it was there.

Carol didn't catch the hint and continued. 'I'm in the Nile. On the Nile. Oh, I'm not sure what the proper grammar is, but the room is lovely. It's like being in an expensive suite of a passenger boat. You'll have to come and have a nosey after dinner.'

Lily knew the correct grammar but decided not to mention it. 'Absolutely,' she said instead. 'You too.'

There's no way Lily would invite a stranger to inspect her living quarters in real life, but here it felt safe, almost normal, even though they'd only just met.

Carol slipped her arm through Lily's and pulled her with surprising strength towards the staircase. 'Let's get a drink. I'm so nervous about meeting everyone, I could do with some fortification.'

They moved a few paces when a flat voice from behind halted them. 'Hello there.'

Lily tried to turn and greet whoever owned it, a challenge with Carol still attached to her arm. The pair rotated as a clumsy unit. A man in an evening suit left the room across the hall. He had dull silver hair, and a somewhat sallow complexion that gave the impression of a lack of sunlight and joy.

Carol didn't seem to notice and, with more enthusiasm than was necessary, dropped Lily's arm to greet him. 'Why, hello.'

Lily held back. If someone had asked her, she couldn't have explained why, but there was something about the way he studied them that made her uncomfortable. Like he was appraising them. Not in a sexual way, more like he was evaluating their worth. Carol wiggled the few steps forwards and shoved her hand out, as she'd done with Lily a few moments ago. Almost practised. She introduced herself and then gestured to Lily, who she described as her 'new friend', which was rather nice.

'Kevin,' he said, a little curt. He took hold of Carol's outstretched hand and brought it up to his lips. 'Charmed.'

Lily gave an involuntary shudder she hoped he didn't see. She didn't offer her own hand.

'Ladies, it would be an honour to escort you both to dinner.' He shoved his elbows out to the side.

Carol giggled as she took hold of one arm and Lily, out of options, did the same. The hallway wasn't wide enough for the three of them to descend in a straight line. Still, she reminded herself, either of these two guests could be the murderer, and she needed to get to know them both as much as she could to give herself the best chance of working that out. Maybe Carol's giggling was a clue. Maybe Kevin was only pretending to be slimy. She determined to find out more, and while she might not enjoy small talk, she'd had plenty of practice from a string of dinners at her parents' house, feigning interest in whatever a potential future husband had to say, and never sure where her mother found the constant supply of unsuitable suitors. She'd rather not know.

With Kevin, she decided to start with something simple. 'How was your journey?'

'Well.' He huffed.

Lily instantly regretted her question, but couldn't take it back now.

Kevin continued, 'Now that you ask, I'm not feeling myself after the ordeal of getting here. The taxi driver was beyond incompetent, and I thought I was going to be late at one point. He needed a satnav to find his way here, if you can believe it.'

Lily thought it both believable and quite reasonable, but kept her opinions to herself. Instead, she concentrated on making her way down the grand stairs, doing her best to keep a gap between her beaded dress and the angular hips of the disagreeable man. She didn't want to miss a clue, so concentrated on every grumbling word he said, while searching around her with what she hoped was subtlety. He was yet to say a single positive thing, preferring to complain and criticise. It would be just her luck to get stuck with him all evening.

At the bottom of the stairs, they reached the drawing room, where a square table held neat rows of glasses filled with a selection of drinks. Behind the table stood a stern butler with a long pale face, wearing a formal black suit, white studded shirt, black waistcoat and bow tie. His icy eyes were a little too close together and Lily couldn't tell if she found his stare professional or intrusive. In either case, he made her uncomfortable.

Kevin dropped their arms and made straight for the table. He peered over the selection to make his choice. Red wine. He took a gulp and lifted the glass to his rejected companions with pure, unadulterated delight on his face.

'Cheers.' He took another glug.

Carol patted her hair. 'Time to go through,' she said, and they shuffled forwards under the supervision of the butler and their host.

'Good evening.' Elliot joined them with a warm smile. 'I see you've made each other's acquaintance. Carol, Lily, allow me to offer you a drink.'

Carol scanned the choices like a child standing in front of a selection of sweets. 'Oh, champagne please.'

The butler passed her a coupe of the decadent drink. She cradled it and gave another giggle as she took a sip. Kevin replaced his now empty wine glass and picked up another, oblivious to the butler.

'Lily.' Elliot spoke to her like she was the only person in the room. 'We've sparkling water, elderflower, orange and apple juice or lemonade.'

Kevin pulled his chin in, but didn't comment, preferring to focus on his wine.

'Sparkling water, please.'

Elliot passed her a tumbler. A slice of lime bounced in the bubbles.

She prepared to explain to the others why she didn't drink. Over the years, she'd found she often needed to justify her choice. Not that there was a specific reason. No religious commitment or troubled history with alcohol. She just didn't particularly like the taste. She primed herself to give her standard justification, when a giant of a man filled the doorway and diverted attention from her. Lily coughed as the bubbles from the water went down the wrong way. She recognised him. How could she not? This was Harvey Bakewell, son of the famous writer Mary Bakewell. Now that was a turn-up.

Harvey hesitated at the entrance to the room. He looked like a nervous gangster, with his bowtie undone around his neck and his braces showing. Mary Bakewell was one of Lily's icons. She'd read all her novels and had even met her once; at a book signing at a local independent bookshop. The last instalment of Mary's detective series had just been released and Lily had patiently queued round the block with the other fans. Although Mary had been autographing copies for well over an hour by the time Lily reached the front of the queue, the writer smiled at her as she asked who to sign the book for, and had made her feel like her wait had been worthwhile. Lily still owned that book. Not long after the event, the author had disappeared from public view.

Harvey shuffled forwards and joined the group. He accepted Elliot's hand to shake as the host made the introductions.

Harvey spoke quickly. All the words pushed together like punctuation was a luxury he couldn't afford. 'Great to meet you all.'

Lily had so many questions for him. 'Great to meet you too, I—'

Kevin cut over her. 'I hear a storm's forecast for tonight. Such an inconvenience.' He took a gulp of wine.

So rude.

'I heard that too.' Carol nodded and waved at the room. 'Still, we'll all be safe in here, and it should have passed by the time we leave. I rather like the idea of being tucked up in an old building listening to the rain.'

'We can only hope, and see what disruption it's left in its wake.' Kevin refused to concede the point. Elliot opened his mouth as if he were about to apologise for the weather, but before she could find out, another guest joined them. One of the most intimidating women Lily had ever seen.

CHAPTER 11

D ebbie surveyed the room. She approached the small group huddled around Elliot Windsor. He was simply marvellous. But, she reminded herself, he wasn't her competition here.

She swept up a drink with a passing thanks to the lanky butler and appraised her rivals, curious to discover what they were made of. 'Good evening,' she said. 'Do you mind if I join you?'

'Not at all,' said the young woman to her side. 'I'm Lily. Nice to meet you.'

She was pretty in a subtle way. Just needed to stand up straight instead of slouching her shoulders.

'Charmed.' She rewarded the girl with a half-smile. 'Debbie Forbes. And who else do we have?' She let the question hang in the air.

Elliot stepped in, taking the hint that his hosting skills were required here. 'Please, let me make the introductions. This is Carol, Kevin, and Harvey.'

'Delighted.' Debbie shook each of their hands.

Carol's eyes widened as she spotted the large, glittering diamond Debbie wore on her right ring finger. She resisted the urge to wipe her palm down her dress after Kevin's limp handshake, and instead she asked, 'How are we all finding the manor? I must say, Mr Windsor, I'm very impressed so far.'

'Elliot, please.' He fiddled with his tie.

An over-excited Carol gripped his arm. 'It's simply wonderful,' she said. 'I just love my room. I've got the Nile, Lily's got Manderley. What theme did you get?'

Debbie wondered if her sales team would be so enthusiastic about interior design. Still, she had to admit, the suite impressed her. 'It's Pyms from *Murder Must Advertise*. I agree, it's terribly clever.'

Elliot coloured at the praise and she rewarded him with her full attention. 'I must say, when Mr McKensey first contacted me, I was sceptical. I wasn't sure a murder mystery weekend would be appropriate for a team-building event, but I'm certainly coming round to the idea. The troops would do well to spend a little more time concentrating on the details, if you know what I mean?'

A circle of blank faces answered her. They clearly didn't know what she meant. They couldn't be from the corporate world, then.

Elliot diverted the conversation again. 'Mr McKensey, Jamie, will join us for dinner.' He checked his pocket watch. 'We've three more guests to come down, then we can make our way through.'

'They'd better hurry up,' Kevin said. 'I'm getting hungry.'

'Quite.' Debbie shut Kevin down and turned her attention to Harvey. 'If you don't mind me asking, you seem familiar. Have we met before?'

Harvey rubbed the side of his face. 'I doubt it. You probably know of my mother, Mary Bakewell.'

'Ah, yes,' Debbie said. 'That's it. The crime writer. Now, doesn't that give you a bit of an unfair advantage?'

'Sadly not. She was the master of mystery. I'm just a car salesman. But she did always say, the clues for any good whodunit should be laid out right at the beginning of the story, when the reader was still settling in and not prepared to spot them yet.'

'Thanks for the tip. And what have you deduced so far?'

Harvey tapped his finger on the side of his nose. 'That would be telling.'

'Fair point. So, what does everyone else do?'

She waited for someone to reply, never one to be afraid of a brief pause in the conversation.

Lily picked at her cuticles. 'I'm in marketing, up in Mayfair.'

Debbie restrained herself from grabbing her hands to make her stop. Instead, she kept her tone upbeat. 'What a coincidence. You're just round the corner from me. We've probably passed each other on the street a hundred times without noticing.'

Debbie sipped her drink. She was enjoying conducting the discussion. 'I rarely leave the office so early, even on a Friday, and the no-technology rule... Now that's going to be a real challenge.' She paused, expecting someone to agree. No one did.

'You must enjoy your job an awful lot.' Carol spoke with what Debbie interpreted as an edge of unnecessary pity in her voice.

'Well, it keeps me busy and out of trouble, so yes, I suppose I do rather enjoy it. Tell me more about you.'

An older couple entered, so the question would have to wait. The woman in a long maroon evening dress and pearl necklace. The man in a traditional three-piece suit and bow tie as the dress code required.

Elliot welcomed them, offering his hand. 'Good evening, Arthur. Grace, I must say, you look simply stunning.'

'Why thank you, dear,' she said.

The group was still busy making introductions when a younger man walked in with a contradictory combination of self-assurance and caution. The last guest. And what a varied bunch it was proving to be. She'd need to choose her team wisely. There was no need to do all the investigations herself if she could delegate. She rather liked chatty Harvey, and he was a strong candidate for a partnership of sorts. Whether she'd let him know that was his role, or what she was doing, was another matter. As Debbie brought her glass up to her lips once more, a gong sounded in the background. Dinner was served.

CHAPTER 12

The gong was Jamie's cue. He could come out of hiding. His stomach made a long, low, gurgling sound. It was time for food and for him to take action. The plan stated he'd only meet the guests this once before the main event. When he and Elliot had made that plan for the weekend, it soon became obvious that for the whole thing to work one of them needed to be front of house and the other behind the scenes. They'd been mid-renovation when Jamie pulled a coin from his overalls and waved it in the air.

'Heads!' Elliot shouted from the top of a ladder across the room. Jamie tossed the coin and checked the answer on the back of his hand.

'You win.' He'd shoved the coin back into his pocket and that had decided it. Elliot would meet the guests as they arrived and he would stay put in the attic, where he could observe the action and amend the game as required. He liked to think of himself as the chess master. Elliot kept reminding him he didn't know how to play chess. Infuriating.

As the screen showed the guests milling through for dinner, he turned his back to them and took the few steps across the square of landing to his bedroom. The springs of the single bed creaked as he balanced on the edge and re-tied the laces of the Oxfords. The old servants' quarters were plain compared to the rest of the house. No need for a theme up here where the guests weren't allowed.

Jamie's room held only the essentials: the bed, a side table holding his e-reader, and a simple full-length mirror propped in the corner. An empty wire coat hanger dangled from a metal hook on the back of the door waiting for the return of his jacket, and a plastic box at the foot of the bed stored props for later. Jamie knew Elliot's room contained more home comforts. He liked to surround himself with pictures of his family and trinkets he'd collected over the years. Jamie, though, preferred the practical and if the weekend didn't require an item, he saw no reason for it to be there. He'd only need to pack it up again and cart it with him later.

Jamie caught his reflection in the mirror. Not so young anymore, and sometimes he worried time would run out. It still seemed like yesterday when the couple he'd been led to believe were his parents sat him down and dropped their double bombshell. They were separating, and he wasn't theirs. Biologically at least. Way to break it to a child easily. And now, over three decades had passed. Some days, he still felt like an unwanted child.

He smoothed his hands down the side of the tweed suit, pulled himself together, and readied himself for his performance. After slipping through the double doors, he took his mark next to Elliot at the head of the table. The heavy curtains were drawn on the world outside and light from two large candelabras flickered from the centre of the table. The guests circled as they searched for their names on the place-holders that would instruct them where to sit.

Debbie pulled back her chair. 'Ah, this is me.'

She flicked open the linen napkin folded in the shape of a fan and settled it on her lap. She raised her hand to the butler in a polite and practised motion. He leaned around her and poured from a bottle of red wine, the neck wrapped in a cloth to prevent any drips. Debbie gave a brief thank you.

Kevin parked himself next to her, clicked in the air and pointed to his own empty glass. 'Some of that here, too.' He already spoke with a slight slur.

The butler poured, unfazed. Debbie didn't bother to hide her disdain, not that Kevin noticed. Jamie, though, hid a smirk.

'Welcome, everyone,' Elliot said. 'Please take your seats.'

The butler manoeuvred around the room with skill, pouring or replenishing drinks.

Max held his hand over the top of the wineglass. 'Not for me, thanks.'
The butler removed the glass by the stem.

'Fancy that.' Lily held up her water. 'Something else we have in common.'

'Cheers.' Max clinked his tall glass with hers.

Jamie took a quick tour of the table and introduced himself.

He lingered next to Carol. 'Good evening.' He held his hands behind his back, leaning forwards as he spoke to her. She smelled like a childhood memory. 'I trust you're settling in and the room's to your liking.'

'Oh yes.' Carol burst with the same enthusiasm he'd watched on the screen, amplified in three dimensions.

The buzz of chatter filled the air, accompanied by soft piano music playing through hidden speakers. Elliot checked his pocket watch. Jamie caught his eye and Elliot rose. He tapped the edge of his glass with his knife. Quite unnecessary, but in keeping with the theatre of the weekend. As Elliot gave another rehearsed speech, Jamie recited the words in his head.

'Thank you again for coming to our inaugural soiree. We do hope you'll enjoy your stay.' He paused for dramatic effect. Perfect. He held their full attention. 'The game has already commenced. We know a crime will be committed. You are the detectives, and your challenge is to find and follow the clues. And now, without further ado, dinner is served.'

The gong sounded again and waiters scurried in carrying bowls of prawn cocktail balanced on silver serving trays. Elliot checked his pocket watch. The fourth time, four more to go.

'How delightfully retro.' Debbie clapped her hands. Harvey glanced at Grace as she selected the smallest silver fork to eat the starter with and did the same. Jamie got the impression he knew which one to use, but somehow doubted himself and didn't want to make a mistake. His mother had famously declared her dedication to details on more than one occasion, so she would have taught him social necessities like this and numerous, less useful customs. Harvey's generous hands enveloped the tiny implement. He chatted to Carol next to him and, while one hand focused on using the delicate fork to move prawns from the dainty bowl, the other swished in front of him as he spoke. 'This is delicious,' he said between scoops.

Carol held her hand over her full mouth. 'I know. I can't remember the last time someone else cooked for me, or when I ate a meal that might contain a potential allergen.'

'That sounds ominous.'

'Not really.' She waved her fork in front of her. 'I'm a childminder, and so many children these days seem to be allergic to this, intolerant to that.'

'Ah, I see.' Harvey laid his miniature fork by the side of the bowl. 'Maybe it's our first clue. That was delicious.'

The waiters cleared the bowls and brought in the next course.

Jamie lifted a spoonful of the rich tomato soup. It reminded him of weekend lunches on winter days, when his father would call him in from playing with the other kids on the street, and heat a can on the stove for them to share between them. The warmth of the soup would vary depending on how long his father stared at the hob, before calling him, and how long it took Jamie to tear himself away from mischief to come inside. He'd always liked it best piping hot.

He addressed Max. 'We were so sorry to hear about Theo's passing. He did so much for the community, but we're pleased you wanted to continue his legacy.'

'Of course.' Max lowered his spoon.

'I'm sorry to hear you've lost someone close.' Lily put her hand next to his on the table, not quite touching. 'He sounds like a wonderful man.'

'He was.' Max took a deep breath. 'He really was the most wonderful man. Set up the youth centre I work in. Helped so many people turn their lives around. Me included. He left me the invite to this weekend as part of my inheritance, if you can believe it. Always determined to find ways to get through, right up to the end.'

Lily tucked her hair behind her ear. 'That's random. How on earth does someone inherit a weekend away?'

Jamie replied. 'We heard Theo's illness was progressing rapidly and contacted him to ask if Max here would be interested in joining our inaugural event on behalf of the youth centre. Our intention long term is to offer deserving charities the option to attend free of charge, so we're hoping to gather feedback on whether that's viable.'

'That's generous of you,' Lily said.

Max stroked the edge of the table. 'He knew I wouldn't come if he just asked me to, so instead he made it a condition of his will.'

'I think I'd have liked Theo.'

'He was easy to like.' Max pushed his bowl away and a silent waiter removed it, scraping away non-existent crumbs.

The fish course was served.

At the far end of the table, Harvey and Carol conferred with their heads close together.

Grace narrowed her eyes. 'You two look like you're plotting something.'

'Oh, no,' Carol said. 'We were just chatting about the pictures.' Jamie bit back a laugh at her feigned innocence.

'Then I'm afraid I'll be forced to make the first confession of the weekend,' Arthur said. 'I know next to nothing about art. My Grace here is the creative one.' He picked up his wife's hand and brought it to his lips.

Jamie found them a little on the sickly sweet side, as a couple.

Max, though, either didn't notice, or didn't mind. 'There are some stunning pieces here. I'd say someone's got a good eye.'

Elliot's neck reddened beneath his bow tie. He'd chosen or commissioned most of the art.

Jamie took a bite of fish. 'Oh yes, I hear you paint, Max. Quite talented, I believe.'

'I wouldn't go that far, but, yes, I do,' he said. 'How did you know that?'

'Lucky guess.' Jamie rested his fork on the side of the plate.

Debbie deflected the discussion away from art. 'Come on, Harvey,' she said, 'what would your mother think of all this? Shall we give her a quick ring and get some hints about how to spot all the clues we've been missing?'

An uncomfortable silence settled around the table. Harvey fiddled with his dessert spoon.

Lily answered for him, in a soft voice. 'Even if we wanted to, we couldn't do that. She's not well.'

'Oh.' Debbie hid her embarrassment admirably. It couldn't be often she made a mistake like that. 'Apologies, I wasn't aware.'

Harvey was gracious. 'It's okay. In her better days, she'd have loved it here.'

'And how is she doing, if it's not too painful to talk about?'

'Not at all,' he said. 'There are good days and bad. The respite people organised for her to stay in a residential home for the weekend. I hope she's okay.'

'Try not to worry,' Jamie said. 'She's being cared for by people who know what they're doing. We've given the home the landline number just in case. Not that there'll be a need for them to call.' He leaned back in his chair. 'Your mother sounds like a formidable woman and it's as if she's prepared you for this weekend your whole life.'

Carol giggled and nudged Harvey with her shoulder. 'I hope you give the rest of us a chance.'

'You're right,' Harvey said. 'Anyway, let's not fixate on that. How did you guys get your tickets?'

Carol beamed. 'Mine was a gift from my son. Such a lovely surprise.'

'I won a competition,' Lily said.

Kevin speared a new potato and shoved it whole into his mouth. 'Same here.'

Elliot checked his pocket watch.

The butler poured more wine.

CHAPTER 13

M ax leaned over and whispered to Lily. 'Have you ever noticed it's always around the main course when the wine kicks in?'

Lily twisted her plate. 'Good point, just like now.'

'Yes. And we can use that to our advantage.' He gave her a sideways glance and ran his finger around the rim of his glass.

Lily joined in, tapping the tips of her own fingers together. 'I like your thinking,' she said. 'We just need to wait until they're all under the influence, then swoop in and solve the case.'

They might have been joking around, but Max tended to agree with Harvey about the opening scenes of a mystery being the most important, and he didn't want to miss anything obvious. Now he was here, he might as well win.

The butler leaned around him, presenting a simple white plate of duck in a rich orange sauce. Max waited for the others to be served, even though Kevin was already tucking in. Grace and Arthur were across the table from him. The older generation fascinated him, and he often found inspiration for his paintings when he listened to their stories.

Grace radiated classic elegance. She had white hair, cropped around the ears where she wore simple pearl studs that matched her long necklace and complemented her stylish maroon dress.

She spotted him staring. 'Yes, dear?' she said, inviting him to speak.

Max wanted to know more about the couple. 'I was just wondering how long you've been married.' He hoped she wouldn't take offence.

'Oh, a very long time, dear.' She tipped her head to the side like she was trying to remember. 'Must be over forty years?' The question hung in the air as a challenge to her husband.

'Forty-six this summer.' Arthur didn't miss a beat, addressing his wife and pretending to be stern. 'As you well know.'

He took her hand and raised it to his lips. He did that a lot. So often Max wondered if he was hiding something and was deflecting.

'Forty-six wonderful years.'

Grace rewarded him with her own loving smile.

'Wow,' said Max. 'And how did you meet?'

Lily leaned forwards on the table. 'Oh yes. Please tell us. I love a good romance, almost as much as a mystery.'

'Well, dear, it's a simple story, I'm afraid. We were barely adults when we met. Arthur had recently joined the police force.' She patted his arm, as if to confirm she meant him. They were a very tactile couple. 'He caught my eye one day doing his beat. Touched his helmet as he walked by, and my heart melted.'

Arthur interjected. 'I had to keep walking. I was with my partner and I couldn't let on how terrified I was, what with such a dazzling woman smiling at me. Real men hid their emotions in those days and I'd have never lived it down if I'd let on.'

Grace picked up the story. 'I went back to that street at the same time every day for a fortnight, and every day, Arthur touched his helmet, and I waited for him to speak to me. Every day he walked by.'

She waited, giving Arthur his opportunity to pick up the thread. Max wondered how many times they'd told this story.

'And do you know, it was the same colleague who suggested that maybe I should "just ask the girl out", and so, on a damp day in April, I pulled myself together and that's exactly what I did. Ended up asking him to be my best man.'

'Such a romantic story.' Lily held her hand to her chest. Max, ever the sceptic, couldn't help but wonder if it was a bit too neat. Possibly even part of the game.

'What about the two of you?' Grace asked. 'Spouses, children?'

Lily tucked her hair behind her ear.

Grace realised she'd struck a nerve and backtracked. 'Plenty of time for all that, dear, and so many women these days live fulfilling lives without a man to take care of. It will happen when you least expect it.'

Grace glanced to the end of the table, where Elliot was busy discussing something serious with Debbie. Lily studied the tablecloth and missed the hint.

Grace carried on, unperturbed. 'You just need to spot the clues. Now where was I? Oh yes. We married in the mid-70s. The time style forgot. The horror of some guests' outfits still haunts our photo album.' She widened her eyes, and Max couldn't help laughing.

'We bought a house. It was still possible to do that in those days on a normal wage. Not like now. Arthur did well in the police force and I worked in a department store until the children came along.'

Max detected the longing in her voice. Once again, Grace pre-empted the question he was still forming in his mind. She must have had this conversation many times before. Justified her choices.

'It was the way things were then. Life blessed us with two wonderful children and I concentrated on caring for the family until they were ready to marry and start families of their own. There was plenty to keep me busy. We used to hold dinner parties with our friends, and the children always needed help with something or other.'

'I still remember the first time you made a prawn cocktail,' Arthur said. 'Nearly poisoned us all. I was so sick, I was forced to take a day off work.' It didn't seem to have left him with any lasting aversion to shellfish if the speed he'd devoured the starter earlier was anything to go by.

'Oh, yes. I've never cooked prawns again.'

Polite laughter made its way around the group.

'I think I spotted you're in the *Mousetrap* room,' Lily said. 'I'd love to hear more about it.'

'Very observant,' Grace said. 'I can tell we're going to have to watch out for you.'

'It's one of our favourite plays,' Arthur said. 'I can't tell you how many times we've been.'

Max knew of it, but had never seen it.

Lily had. 'I saw it when it toured. The local theatre was packed. Inspirational. And a bit like Kendrick Manor, I suppose. We'll all know the outcome in a few days, and it'll be our secret.'

Grace agreed. 'Yes, that's a fair point. This whole thing makes you think, well, it does me. What would it be like to commit a murder and, more importantly, would you get away with it?'

She dabbed her napkin at the side of her mouth. She was joking. Max was sure she was joking. But then, appearances weren't always what they appeared to be.

CHAPTER 14

T his wasn't like any dinner party Debbie had frequented before, and it was proving to be a lot more fun. A complete hotchpotch of people populated the table, none of whom she'd give a passing thought to in normal life, let alone engage in social niceties with. As she wiped her plate with the last piece of duck, Debbie judged the food to be on a par with restaurants she took clients to, and the wine was superb.

Kevin didn't appear to be equipped with the same level of tolerance for it as she was. When he spoke, slurring some comment or criticism, little drops of spit escaped. He hacked at his duck and chomped on it. He wiped a dribble of sauce from his chin with his sleeve. Revolting.

Debbie's rule was simple when interacting with the 'general population', as she liked to refer to them, and by that, she meant those that neither worked in nor understood the corporate world. That rule was to be purposely vague about her line of work. She'd learned a long time ago that people who didn't work in the industry simply didn't understand either what she did or why she found it so satisfying, so it was best to skirt the details. These people took lunch-breaks and had hobbies, for pity's sake. No, when asked, it was far easier to deflect the exchange back to the other person as quickly as possible and, if they persisted, to baffle them with corporate jargon.

Kevin asked the obvious question, his mouth still full of duck. 'What line of work are you in?' It appeared she had limited choice.

'I'm Sales and Marketing Director for a Global Technology Firm in the West End.' She gave him a beat, waiting to see if he'd ask anything further, and then changed the subject. 'This wine's delicious.' She held her glass by the stem, swirled the contents, and inhaled the scent. 'I wonder what vintage it is.'

'Not sure it matters.'

It was obvious he didn't have any knowledge about quality wine. He bounced the conversational ball right back to her, asking a question of his own. Maybe he was less drunk than she'd thought, or possessed more intelligence than she'd given him credit for. He asked about her family; she asked about his. They covered jobs, hobbies, favourite TV shows, the journey to the manor and even the weather.

Yes, he was good. Annoying, and a tad vulgar, but she couldn't deny he was proving to be a gifted sparring partner. Debbie locked eyes with Lily, and the two women exchanged a knowing glance that Kevin didn't catch. Now there was someone she was keen to get to know more about.

The butler stopped, waiting to be called over to replenish Kevin's wine and topped it up each time he passed.

Although she enjoyed sparring with Kevin for a short while, Debbie soon tired of him. She didn't want to spend the entire meal talking to the same person. Time to broaden her network. Kevin reclined in his chair, replete.

Debbie took the opportunity and leaned forwards to speak with the girl. 'Hello again,' she said. 'Lily, isn't it?'

The girl fidgeted on the spot and gave her an almost imperceptible nod. 'Hi. Yes, that's me.'

Debbie wondered about her. Capability wasn't always aligned to extroversion, and this quiet, but self-assured, woman had something about her that implied exactitude. She cut each piece of food into precise squares before chewing, as if she were intent on discovering the hidden joy in each mouthful.

'How's your room?'

Lily might have started with generic small talk, but it made a change from the standard and often awkward topic of career. Curious, and rather refreshing.

'I have to say, I'm impressed,' Debbie said. 'It's expertly done. There's a spiral staircase in the corner and the most exquisite vintage typewriter. Your turn, how's yours?'

'I'm going to be dreaming in Manderley.' Lily spoke in a wistful tone as she performed a variation of the famous opening line. It had been years since Debbie read the novel, but the Gothic setting came flooding back to her. Until 'the question' came.

'And what do you do?' Lily sipped her water.

Debbie provided the same answer she'd given Kevin, who, she noted, seemed to be on the verge of dozing off between the two of them. His head dropped forwards, and he opened his eyes, startled, then closed them again.

Lily, to her credit, ignored him and continued their conversation. 'Oh yes, you mentioned you work in the West End. I work for an IT company in Mayfair too. Nowhere near as important as you, though. I work in the comms team.'

Debbie could imagine that. An employee more comfortable putting words down on paper than they were using them to drive the business forwards. Still, it didn't do well to underestimate the value of these people.

Kevin's head bounced to his chest as he tried to stay awake.

Debbie ducked forwards. 'I'll let you in on a little secret,' she said. 'It's all just a game. If you pretend like you know what you're doing, people generally take it for granted that you do.' She gave the girl a wide, warm smile. 'Fake it until you make it and all that.'

Lily put her cutlery together on the plate. 'I'll tell you a secret too,' she said, without looking up. 'I'm having a lovely evening, but I'm a bit disappointed no one's died yet.'

Debbie threw back her head and laughed. How marvellous! Even Kevin, half-asleep between them, snorted.

At the top of the table, Elliot checked his pocket watch. Debbie could have sworn he'd done that not so long ago. She detested unnecessary clock-watching during dinner. Maybe Lily wouldn't have to wait much longer for the murder after all. He was pretending not to, but she was sure he was watching them, or rather, watching Lily. Sweet, innocent Lily. Assuming that wasn't part of her character for the weekend. She'd get chewed up and spat out again in the real world. Debbie's world.

As the waiters cleared the plates, Debbie appraised the guests once more. A hotchpotch, yes, but an interesting collection. All of them hiding something. Everyone harboured their little secrets, and it was always worth taking the time to uncover them. Wonderful what one could use as leverage if you knew how to apply just the right amount of pressure at precisely the right time. She folded her napkin and placed it next to the plate.

Night drew on. The waiters tidied the table and served coffee. Grace muffled a yawn.

Arthur took his cue and stood with an exaggerated groan. 'We'll leave you young people to enjoy the rest of your evening,' he said. 'We've always been larks and us pensioners need our rest.'

Debbie suspected they were off to collate their findings so far. It's what she'd do if she had a partner here. As the only couple, they had a clear advantage. They'd know whether one of them was the murderer and they could gather twice as much evidence. Not what you'd call a level playing field, but then there was no such thing.

Elliot contorted his face, holding back a yawn of his own.

'You can head up too if you like,' Jamie said. 'I'm happy to stay with anyone who wants to join me for a brandy.'

Debbie could have stayed up into the small hours if she'd wanted to. Like all the prominent leaders throughout history, she prided herself on her limited need for sleep. Still, there was nothing to be gained by doing so if most of the others were going to bed. She'd gathered a reasonable understanding of each of them and wanted to note down her thoughts. No murder yet, regrettably.

Harvey was the only one to take Jamie up on his offer, and the two men passed through the double doors back to the drawing room. She left them to it. Soft moonlight shone through the frosted window as she made her way up the wide staircase. With her laptop and phone locked away, she had nothing to do except enjoy a peaceful night's sleep. The grandfather clock ticked in the hallway. Tomorrow, she was sure, there would be a murder.

Morning was just thinking about making an appearance as Debbie stretched out in the comfortable bed. She exhaled in satisfaction and slipped her arm out from under the duvet, reaching for her phone, and then pulled back, as she remembered she'd locked away both her phone and her laptop in the safe. She twisted her head on the pillow and considered the wardrobe, debating whether she should retrieve the phone and tap out a few quick emails. It wasn't like anyone would know she'd flouted their rule. On the other hand, it was refreshing not being contactable. She'd heard stories about executives going on retreats where they waxed lyrical about their experience of a 'digital detox'. She'd always been sceptical. But maybe there was something in it after all.

She felt a strange pride that she'd managed nearly twelve hours technology free. And to think, she'd struggled to choose a number for the safe. Silly when she thought about it; it was just a code. For some reason, she'd been compelled to use a memorable date and deciding which one to choose felt disproportionately momentous. Ridiculous. In the end, she'd chosen her first day at this current job, the day she'd walked into the office and almost tasted the pressure and exhilaration in the air from a hundred workers judging her.

Hard to believe it was coming up on four years since she'd made that entrance. Now the office was unrecognisable. She remembered the battered desks crammed together, so close the screens on top touched. There'd been a buzz in the air, people on the phone, speaking into headsets, some standing, some sitting furiously typing. Most desks held two screens, as if it weren't possible to get all the work done on a single one. Some even had three. None of them matched and all of them needed a good clean. The hum of concentrated noise ceased as soon as she'd entered, like someone had pressed mute on the world.

Debbie had walked purposefully through them. She always walked with purpose. Heels high, shoulders back, pace, not haste. She wasn't the first female director they'd ever had, just the youngest, and head-hunting her from one of their biggest competitors was considered both a triumph and a break from convention. She'd been told they normally liked to 'grow their own'. The CEO had been irritatingly proud of that when he interviewed her, but she was there because they were haemorrhaging clients and, in fairness, he knew they needed to shake things up if they stood any chance of survival.

Debbie would never admit it, but she'd been flattered they'd chosen her and a bit overwhelmed. It was her biggest secret. The company was huge, and she pushed her impostor syndrome to one side as she strode across the floor and into the corner office they'd allocated her. She slipped her leather satchel to the floor under the desk and switched on the computer. Milly popped her head around the door to introduce herself as her PA and to ask if she'd like a drink. Debbie's attention flicked up to Milly, young, vibrant and wearing far too much make-up. She'd inherited her from her predecessor and intended to make a quick evaluation of her ability before she decided whether or not to keep her. Milly adjusted and dropped her gaze in submission, while simultaneously standing her ground.

'Coffee. Thank you.' Debbie switched her attention back to her screen.

Milly retreated. Already clear they would not be bonding. When she'd brought the instant coffee in a beige plastic cup, Debbie took a sip and winced.

She passed Milly a platinum credit card. 'We'll start with buying a decent coffee machine.'

In the years that followed, Debbie proved the CEO right. She'd worked tirelessly since that first day and driven the sales figures up until they were the highest in the company's history, and the firm was not only safe, but thriving. She restructured. Stripped out the lazy, incompetent, and obsolete. She improved conditions for those who remained. Provided breakout areas, with sofas, and proper tea and coffee replaced the machine. She arranged for breakfast-making facilities to be installed and fruit baskets to be delivered, knowing if she fed the workers, they'd be more productive and at their desks earlier. Her staff cull hadn't been personal. She'd been impartial when she reviewed the data and instructed HR based on the facts. The clients loved her. The team admired her, even if they were a little intimidated, which was just as it should be. Milly proved to be diligent and capable. She often asked if Debbie needed anything, but never tried to befriend her again. Most agreeable.

Debbie rarely allowed herself the luxury of doing nothing, and yet it was a strangely freeing experience to just lie in bed for a while, safe in the knowledge that no one could contact her. Her team, her bosses, the partners, on both sides of the world, would have to cope without her for the next couple of days. She wriggled her shoulders. It would be character building for them, and she would enjoy observing how they managed. There would be consequences for those that couldn't.

Without early morning work to occupy her, Debbie pushed herself up in bed, flicked on the table lamp and took in the details of the room, sure there must be clues. As she'd told Lily the night before, the theme of her room was the famous Dorothy Sayers novel, *Murder Must Advertise*, where, if she remembered correctly, the protagonist went undercover to expose a drug plot. The novel inspired the decor of this room. How quaint. As someone who prided herself on her meticulous attention to detail, Debbie appreciated the touches that made this room unique.

Unused to inactivity, she grew bored and abandoned her decision to stay in bed, in favour of noting down her observations from the night before. She swung her long legs out from under the covers and slipped on her silk robe. She padded barefoot to the desk and lowered herself into the leather executive chair that rocked beneath her. Her fingers settled on the round, black keys of the typewriter, and she reflected on the contrast between her own subtle manicure and the brash red favoured by Carol. Unless Debbie was mistaken, and she very rarely was, she was definitely a woman with a secret.

Then there was Kevin, crass and clearly unused to being in polite society. Each time he'd waved the butler over to replenish his drink, Debbie had cringed at the commonality of the gesture. She'd always been able to hold her drink. It might not be stipulated in her job description, but it was an important part of her role to wine and dine, and still be able to put in effective hours at the office. She noted Kevin had failed to show similar skill the night before. He'd practically fallen asleep at the table, for pity's sake. Oh, and his complaining, how exhausting to listen to him recall his journey in intricate detail and the supposed horror of a minicab driver who dared not to be British and had the gall to use a navigation device to make sure his passenger reached his desired destination. She abhorred prejudice. In her view, there was simply no place for it in the modern economy. She'd found Kevin to be a loathsome little man. He'd referenced a wife who, from the sounds of it, was enjoying her own pleasurable weekend in the company of outdoorsy types. Good for her.

Debbie added a fresh sheet of paper to the typewriter. Lily worked in the same part of London as she did. She reminded her of Milly: young, sparky, full of hope and aspiration. Less confident, though. Shame.

Max had inked his story on his skin. She'd like to find out more about that. She'd always admired other people's tattoos, even if she'd never been brave enough to get one herself. Yes, her initial impressions were giving her some insight into her competition, but there was still more to do. She'd use today to gain influence and draw out those secrets, fully intending to win this weekend. Winning was what she did.

Debbie checked the time on the wind-up clock on the bedside table. The plethora of clocks scattered about was a nice touch in a property that asked its patrons to lock away their devices. She made a note, in case it was significant.

In the bathroom, miniature bottles of luxury products lined up with their labels facing forwards. She took a refreshing shower, wrapped herself in a soft, white towel, and then dressed in designer jeans and a loose cashmere sweater. She opted for fresh rather than instant coffee, as she always did, and headed out of the room to find some.

On the landing, a lone portrait hung on the wall. A vintage piece, painted in oil and surrounded by a golden frame. The resemblance to Elliot struck her. Mesmerised, she crossed her arms as she searched the painting for details. The resemblance was uncanny. Could be an ancestor. She'd ask their host about it over breakfast. The potted history she'd read in her room the night before provided a high-level overview of the two hosts and their backgrounds, but nothing about how they'd been able to afford to buy and renovate the manor. She, for one, found that fascinating. Neither of them struck her as old money, although she could be wrong; it did happen on occasion. Elliot might speak like gentry, but he just didn't move like a man who'd been born into money. She could always tell.

The house creaked as the other guests woke and moved around. The door across from hers opened. Arthur and Grace had professed to be larks, so she was surprised to find them leaving their room this late. She supposed it might take them longer to get going in the morning without the structure of a daily commute and the deadlines that defined her own routine.

'Good morning,' Arthur said, a little too peppy for her liking.

She needed her coffee. Still, there was nothing to gain by being rude.

'Good morning,' she said.

The couple had a country gentility about them. Impeccable manners and smartly attired. Arthur in a navy tweed suit, with sharp lines pressed into the front of his trousers and a crisp white shirt open at the neck.

Grace wore a caramel knitted dress, with a pink scarf that shouldn't go, but did. 'Did you sleep well, dear?'

'Yes, thank you.'

As someone who normally woke multiple times in the night to jot down things she needed to do the next day, Debbie wasn't used to sleeping well. She didn't share the novelty, and instead asked the same of them, as manners required in these situations. She marvelled at how people spent their whole lives with one another. She wasn't sure she'd have the patience.

Grace adjusted her scarf. 'Oh yes. We've been up for a few hours, reading and collating our thoughts from last night. Such a delicious dinner, we couldn't fault it. I can't help wondering when the murder is going to be committed, though. There won't be much time to deduce the culprit if it doesn't happen soon.'

Debbie agreed. At this rate, they'd all be packing to go home before they worked out the mystery. She returned her attention to the painting, interested in getting a second opinion.

'Don't you think this portrait has an uncanny resemblance to Elliot?'

Arthur pulled a pair of spectacles from his inside pocket and peered at the oiled image. 'Hmm, so it does. We must ask him about it when he comes down for breakfast. Not sure about your room, but we had a summary of the house's history in ours. It didn't include any information on how the chaps came to own it, or how they raised the capital to build this experience.'

'I suppose it might have been one of those crowdfunding things,' Grace said.

Debbie hesitated, a little lost for words.

Grace tipped her head to the side, giving her a knowing smile. 'Not all retirees are completely out of touch with what's going on today, dear.'

Apparently, there was more to Grace than years of being a housewife. Interesting. Debbie found them pleasant enough. Easy to talk to, with a natural understanding of where the social barriers lay, which, after her experience with Kevin last night, was a welcome reprieve.

'We were about to head downstairs and see who else is up and about,' Arthur said.

Grace slipped her arm through his and Debbie followed just behind. The stairway was wide, but there was no need for them all to cram together, and it was easy enough to continue their chat. The door to the drawing room was closed when they reached it.

Arthur stepped forwards. 'Let me.'

He pulled the door open and stood politely to one side, allowing the women to pass first. How gallant. How unnecessary. Grace gave him an adoring gaze as she passed. She screamed. Debbie, just behind her, held back a gasp of her own. Jamie, still dressed in his tweed suit, lay face down on the Oriental rug, surrounded by a crimson pool. A hammer rested at his side. The murder of Kendrick Manor had been committed.

CHAPTER 15

L ily poured her tea. Earl Grey, her favourite, and it always tasted better in a
china cup. The sash window of her room looked out over the rose garden
and the low winter sun shone through the pieces of paper she'd taped to the
panels. The character sheets might obstruct the view, but she'd not wanted to
risk ruining the delicate floral wallpaper and this way she could hide her musings
behind the curtains if she needed to.

She'd dressed in skinny jeans and an oversized sweater with the sleeves rolled
up around the wrists. She'd made the bed. The room was tidy, just as she liked
things to be.

She took a new sheet of paper from the pad and printed 'HARVEY
BAKEWELL' in pencil at the top. Lily knew lots about his mother, a staunch
activist for women's rights and one of the most prolific writers of her generation.
Her memoir documented her struggles as a single mother, how she'd balanced
the desire to love and support her child in a society that frowned upon un-
married women. When she'd received her diagnosis, she'd shifted her focus to
challenging the stigma associated with early onset dementia. A fascinating and
inspiring story, if tinged with sadness.

But Lily didn't know much about the man himself. For someone who talked
so much, he said very little. Lily patted the pencil against her lip. It could be a
tactic, or it could just be the way he was. She wasn't sure, but she needed to be
careful not to judge him based on his mother. Maybe the fast talking was the

clue. Her own instructions had suggested she look at the ground frequently, not too much bother for someone naturally on the shy side.

She tried another approach and titled a fresh sheet of paper 'CLUES'. Not everything could be about character. Elliot's pocket watch could be something. He checked it often enough. Lily peeked through the gap in the sheets of paper. A sparrow flew past.

A high-pitched, piercing scream worthy of a Hitchcock actress travelled through the manor and Lily's head flicked round to the closed door. She dropped the pencil. Her skin tingled. This was it. Act two. Time to progress with the investigation. She slipped on her shoes and hurried downstairs to find the source of the scream.

She peered around the half open drawing room door. The curtains were closed, and the chandelier cast a warm yellow light on the murder scene. A cobweb clung to its branches. Debbie, Grace and Arthur stood guard over Jamie's twisted body.

None of them acknowledged her as she joined their vigil. Lily's logical mind reminded her once again that this was a staged murder. A game. But the contrast of her memory of Jamie's animated humour the night before and his stillness now was stark. It didn't look staged. It looked real. He lay on his front with his arms and legs at awkward angles that couldn't be comfortable. He'd created the perfect shape for someone to mark white tape around. A blood halo surrounded his head.

Debbie held her hands behind her back and paced, measured steps moving back and forth along the wall in front of the mantelpiece. Arthur pulled a black notepad from his inside pocket, flipped the top, and scribbled something. He showed it to Grace, who placed her hand on his arm in silent agreement.

Kevin stumbled in. He wore a pair of tartan pyjamas and corduroy slippers. He rubbed his already dishevelled hair. 'What's all the noise?' His words were still slurred from the night before. His red eyes widened. 'Oh.' As he rubbed his hand through his hair again, a cough came from behind him.

Kevin moved aside to let Harvey in. At least he'd bothered to get dressed. Jeans and a blue shirt, tucked in, and held with a brown leather belt stretched around his middle.

Harvey licked his lips and his eyes gleamed. 'Well, here we go, then. We're all officially suspects in the murder of Jamie McKensey.'

Debbie stopped pacing and put her hands on her hips. 'You were the last person to see him alive.'

'No,' Harvey said. 'The killer was the last person to see him alive.'

Lily nibbled her bottom lip. Nicely done, Harvey.

Carol slid into the room and stood next to her new ally in solidarity. Harvey was by far the most comfortable with his investigation, and they'd only just got underway. Lily needed to focus. The clock was ticking, literally and figuratively. With the grand reveal scheduled for that evening, time was tight to work out the puzzle, and she needed to compare the clues she'd picked up so far with the crime. The group shuffled around the scene like they were practising a dance.

Max appeared and stood in the far corner, alone. Lily watched as he observed the room, his eyes darting between the victim, the guests, and the exit. His enthusiastic humour the day before replaced by a drawn, pained expression. Maybe he'd been up all night murdering Jamie, and his exhausted appearance was his confession. She couldn't assume, just because they'd struck up a friendship of sorts, that he hadn't hidden his murderous tendencies. As he spotted her, his face softened and some of the tension seemed to leave his shoulders. No, she couldn't rationalise it. She just couldn't imagine him as the killer.

Debbie morphed into some sort of automated corporate leader. She slipped her hands into her pockets and started pacing again. She never seemed to switch off, and while she was nice enough as a whole, Lily found her domineering approach exhausting.

'We must all pull together to uncover the murderer,' she said in a voice that was just a fraction louder than necessary. Like she was commanding that team of hers and any hint of disagreement would not be tolerated.

Arthur, however, had his own ideas. 'Young lady, I think you'll find that this is not a team sport. It's a competition.'

'Quite right, dear.' Grace tucked her arm through his.

Debbie, not used to opposition, pulled her chin into her neck. This charming, old-fashioned retiree was also used to being listened to, even if his command came with a dash more subtlety than hers did.

'Without wishing to offend, Grace and I have no desire to expand our group. *You* are, of course, welcome to join forces if you choose.' Lily stifled a giggle. Debbie pursed her lips. It never did well to underestimate the older generation. Maybe that would teach her to be a little less condescending. Score one for Arthur, and Lily suspected there was much more to Grace than she let on. They had a game plan, too.

Debate started. Opinions and assumptions overlapped with allegations and denials. Lily tucked her hair behind her ear and took a step back. She didn't want to be part of this. She'd be more efficient if she could reflect somewhere quiet. She edged backwards and left them to it.

Lily scurried along the black and white tiled hall to the conservatory. It was warm and bright; the glass panels framed the brilliant blue sky. Much better. She didn't know much about architecture, but even she could tell this was a later addition to the manor. Floor to ceiling windows revealed the rose garden and gave a different perspective from the view she'd enjoyed from her room. A breakfast buffet waited under the silver domes of traditional chafing dishes. She weaved through square tables covered in lace tablecloths, drawn by the aroma of the cooked bacon.

Lily selected an individual silver pot, added a tea bag, and let the hot water from the urn scorch the leaves. While it brewed, she browsed through the selection of fresh fruit, bread, and hot and cold meat, choosing a modest breakfast of cereal and an orange. It might smell amazing, but she was still full from last night's feast. Footsteps alerted her to a companion.

'Morning,' Max said. He stood by her side. 'Any ideas?'

'A few,' she said. 'You?'

'A couple.' He picked up a plate from the warmer and filled it with a cooked breakfast. Sausage, bacon, egg and hash brown. She didn't know how he could manage all that.

Lily prompted. 'An elderly couple?'

'Maybe.'

Lily chose a table by the window and settled the napkin on her lap. She poured her tea and added a dash of milk from a small ceramic jug, leaving it next to the pretty vase that held a silk flower. Max scraped a chair back. All jokes aside, she was keen to find out more about most of the guests, but Grace and Arthur intrigued her the most. She could also do with some fresh air and wanted to explore the grounds before the supposed storm arrived later. Not that there was any way to check the forecast without breaking the no-technology rule.

Max sliced his bacon. Lily peeled the orange. The hall door swung open. Grace's arm looped through Arthur's as always, their heads close together, like they were discussing the weekend's events so far and their theories.

Max called out and gestured to the two empty seats. 'Plenty of space at our table.'

It would be the perfect chance to find out a bit more about them. Well done him. Lily had enjoyed Arthur's stories last night, about his time as a young police officer. She could picture him coming home from work and discussing his current case with his wife. There'd be regulations about that these days, but as they'd said themselves, they were from a different time.

'We'd be delighted, dear.' Grace dropped Arthur's arm and inspected the breakfast offering.

Arthur used a serviette to pick up a plate from the warmer. He fumbled with the metal tongs and reached towards a pile of sausages. Grace flicked her own napkin at him. He smiled at her scolding and took the breakfast, anyway. You didn't need to be a detective to guess this was a departure from his normal diet and he intended to take full advantage of the opportunity.

Arthur carried his plate over and put it on the table. He gave them a conspiratorial wink.

'It'll be back to porridge on Monday, so I'm going to enjoy this while I can.'

He'd hardly loaded up a breakfast of a man destined for obesity: a couple of sausages, a slice of bacon, and grilled tomatoes. But, at his age, maybe his doctor might disapprove as much as his wife.

Max rose from the table. 'Smells fabulous. I think I should probably get some bacon, just to check. Wouldn't want to find out someone's poisoned the food.'

'What *are* you talking about?' Arthur pulled a chair out for Grace.

She settled her own breakfast selection on the table: granola and yoghurt. Ever the diplomat, her voice was smooth and patient. 'He's teasing you, dear.' She patted her husband's arm.

'Yes,' Lily said, 'and he's already had some bacon, so he's just using it as an excuse to go back for seconds.'

'Ah, guilty as charged.' Max took his plate, still half full, and added more bacon from the dish.

'You're an unlikely partnership,' Grace said, 'but I approve.'

'Oh, we're not...' Lily started to reply, then thought better of it and took another mouthful of cereal instead.

Grace ate slowly while Arthur tucked in. He looked up between bites, clearly considering if whether he could go back for a second helping.

Grace saw it too. 'Maybe some fruit, dear. We don't want you having a heart attack.'

Arthur ignored the suggestion of fruit, hiding his disappointment behind their investigation. 'So,' he said. 'Not sure about you young people, but I'm fascinated to know how Jamie stayed so still.'

Lily put her spoon down in her now empty bowl. 'Not sure, but it's brilliant. He even hid his breathing. He must have been there all night, waiting for us to discover him. I wonder if they'll close up the room after the search. He can't stay there for the rest of the weekend.'

'Fair point,' Max said. 'It seems to have been set up as the focal room, although maybe that's a clue, and was just meant to hint to us the murder was going to be committed in there.'

Lily topped up her tea. 'Could be. Mystery stories are normally structured around the characters, or the location as a whole, rather than just a room. It doesn't mean this one isn't. It's just less likely.'

'How come you know so much about mystery?' Max said.

She wasn't sure if he was interviewing her, but she humoured him for now. 'I've just always enjoyed reading and working out puzzles,' she said. 'When I was little, Mum used to take us to the library.'

'Us?' Arthur said.

'Don't interrupt, dear.'

Lily grinned. 'Yes, me and my sister. She hated it, acted like it was a punishment. Oh, but I loved it there. Loved the old paper smell and the quiet. I used to choose a different shelf of the library each week and pick out three books to borrow. I'd read anything and loved them all. Like most kids, I suppose. Before they start to believe reading isn't cool.' She gave a self-depreciating laugh while she fiddled with her napkin.

'Reading *is* cool,' Max said. 'I was the same with drawing, used to hide my notebooks under the bed.'

'I shared a room, so there wasn't much chance of that. My sister saw the stacks of books and the time I spent devouring them. In fairness, she never teased me. Just didn't get the fascination. I always assumed it was because she was older, more popular.' She looked up.

'Go on,' said Grace with an encouraging smile.

Lily shrugged. 'Anyway, some of those books must have been mystery novels. I remember reading all the old classics – Nancy Drew, the Famous Five – and somewhere along the way, they became adult mystery novels. I still read everything, but those are my favourites.'

'I regret not reading more when I was a kid,' Max said. 'Spent too much time hanging around on street corners, avoiding being at home. Books were another thing Theo introduced me to. The youth centre had a library room. Nothing fancy like the one here, just a converted boxroom with mismatched bookcases along the walls, stuffed with donations. All different colours and sizes of MDF, stuffed with books in no particular order. Although the kids could borrow them, I never did. I used to read them when I was there, curled up in the corner. Sometimes, I'd begin a book and when I came back a few days later, someone else had borrowed it, so I'd have to wait for them to bring it back before I could read the rest.'

Lily covered her mouth with a playful gasp.

'It worked for me, meant I got to escape into a different world and never needed to worry about whether I was stopping someone else doing the same.'

'I don't know how you did it. I wouldn't have had the patience,' Lily said. 'I had enough trouble making sure I finished all my library books before they were due back. I always borrowed more than I could read in two weeks.'

'Looking back, I think Theo probably intervened. The book I was part way through was still there more often than not.'

'I'm so sorry for your loss, Max,' Grace said. 'Did I hear Jamie mention Theo organised your invite here?'

Max took a bite of toast. 'Sort of. He was always being gifted tokens of thanks from people or charities he supported. I didn't even recognise the name of this one. It just arrived one day, a fancy brochure, a ticket, and a typewritten letter.'

'Ours was the same,' Arthur said.

Max rubbed his hand up his arm. 'To be honest, by then, Theo's care was palliative, so there was no way he could've attended personally.'

'You're lucky to have found a friend so dedicated to you.' Grace spoke with sincerity. 'He sounds like a wonderful man, and I'm sure he'd be proud of you for having the courage to attend this weekend when you're still grieving. It's what he wanted.'

'There's no mystery there,' Max said. 'He was always telling me I needed to get out more and meet people. Learn to trust, blah, blah.' He waved away the memory.

Grace appreciated the irony. 'So he sent you to a murder mystery weekend where you know for sure someone's lying and the whole point is to not trust people. That's brilliant.'

'Anyway, this isn't furthering our investigation. We should focus.' Max studied Grace, leaning forwards. 'Where were you at the time of the murder?'

Grace played along. 'Why, Max,' she said incredulously. 'We went to bed early. Remember? We were fast asleep. And anyway, we could ask you the same thing. Without wanting to offend, you do seem a bit tired.'

Max leaned back again in his chair and folded his arms. 'Side effect of grief,' he said, 'but I promise I didn't get up in the night to go on a killing spree. So, Lily, fancy testing out your theory? See if Jamie is still in the drawing room or if they've closed it off?'

'Share our clues and combine forces to work out who the murderer is?' she said. 'Nice try, Max. I don't think so. There can only be one winner, so if you all don't mind, I think I'll leave you to it. I could do with some fresh air while there's a break in the rain.'

She carried her empty breakfast things to the collection space, leaving the table of three.

As Lily moved away, she heard Arthur say, 'Funny girl.'

'She's just a bit of a loner,' Grace said.

'It's the quiet ones you need to watch out for. They're the ones who'll get away with murder when you're not paying attention.'

Lily didn't hear any more. The door closed behind her.

CHAPTER 16

Lily buttoned up her coat and wound her scarf around her neck. She was glad to be outside and to get some fresh air, despite the chill. The pebble paths wound through the rose garden and shone in the damp. The rain held off for now. A few determined flowers clung to the branches, twisting around the trellis. White wooden benches, normally tucked away under a canopy of blossom, were clearly on display as they waited for summer to return. Until then, the garden prepared to hibernate. It was magical.

Lily expected to be alone in the garden, but as she rounded a corner, she saw Harvey ensconced on a bench with his back to the house. She wondered where Carol was. They'd already become a detecting duo. Her feet crunched on the pebbles and he spotted her, giving her a small smile that didn't quite fit his face.

'Care to join me?' he asked.

Lily pulled off her glove and patted the seat first. Despite the branches being bare, the nook still gave the illusion of privacy, but she was sure if anyone bothered, they could watch them from the house. The two of them relaxed in comfortable silence for a while, their shoulders touching, the slight warmth of sunshine on their faces, both thinking their own thoughts.

Even though they were still in London, she was amazed how quiet it was. No hum of traffic or people chattering, just the occasional bird and soft rustle of trees in the breeze.

Lily loved being outside. She'd been forced to spend so much of her childhood stuck indoors that now she craved nature. Her parents had considered it dangerous to play out on the street with the other children, and her sister always refused to join her in the small family back garden, a simple patch of pristine, if plain, grass. She'd felt self-conscious out there on her own, until she'd discovered that if she took a book, she had a reason to be there. The library story she'd told at breakfast was only part of it. Her freedom and creativity were cultivated outside. Even now, she often came up with her best ideas when she was walking. She dreamed that, one day, she'd save up enough money to buy a simple cottage in the countryside, where she could spend all her time writing, walking, and dreaming. No dreaming just now, though.

Harvey shifted, and the bench creaked. 'A little bird told me you're an aspiring writer,' he said. 'Mum would be pleased there's a new generation coming through.'

'I was sorry to read the news about her illness,' Lily said. 'Do you look after her full-time?'

'I do,' he said. 'There's help, of course – nurses, friends, but mostly it's just me and her.' He waved his hand in front of him, dispersing the topic. 'Anyway, let's not talk about that now. Tell me more about your stories and how you come up with your ideas.'

Lily pushed a curved line into a pile of damp leaves with the toe of her shoe. 'I always work on the characters first, and then the plot just kind of develops from how they'd react in that set of circumstances. I've been wondering if Elliot and Jamie did the same here. There's no reason to expect they created a single plot and intend to recycle it each time they run the weekend. They could just as easily build the crime around the guests. Maybe that's why Jamie didn't meet us until dinner.'

'Interesting theory.'

Harvey rubbed the side of his face. He was waiting for her to say more, interviewing her. Like she wouldn't notice. She'd need to be careful not to give away her suspicions.

'I'm curious what you make of our hosts, Harvey. How do they stack up as characters?'

'I didn't speak to Jamie much before he, well, you know. Elliot strikes me as nice enough, though, and they've done wonders with the manor.'

Harvey lifted his hand to his face again, faltered, and lowered it back down. Strange. Sometimes when you spoke to him, you got a stream of consciousness. Other times, he needed to be prompted. Like his control of speech was his protective shield. What he'd said didn't make sense. He'd been the only guest to stay up last night, drinking brandy with Jamie after the others had all gone to bed, so he must have talked to him. It could be a clue.

Harvey continued, 'We're all hiding things, from our real lives and for the weekend. I'm still not sure what's connected to the murder. You've spotted the theme, I assume?' He stared straight ahead as he asked his question, as if facing her would stop her from answering.

'Oh, yes,' she said, truthfully.

Harvey patted his knees. 'Well, I could sit out here all day, enjoying your company, but we won't be in for a chance of winning if we do.'

He extracted himself from the bench and offered Lily his hand. It encased hers as he pulled her up with a gentleness she wouldn't have expected from someone his size.

The sun disappeared and Lily shivered, but she wasn't ready to go back inside yet. 'There's a storm forecast for tonight. I think I'll take a quick walk around the grounds before it gets here.'

'Better be quick.' Harvey pointed to the sky. 'Those clouds look ominous.'

Lily watched him meander through the light drizzle towards the conservatory.

She agreed with Harvey. She wouldn't have long. The wind picked up and brought with it the dark clouds that had clung to the horizon all morning. Lily wrapped her arms around her middle and ducked under a stone arch that marked the threshold between the rose garden and the grounds. The immaculate lawn extended out until it reached a muddy bank on one side, where erosion exposed the roots of an ancient tree. Shrubs lined the curved path that invited exploration. Lily obliged.

As she strolled away from the manor, Lily considered what she knew so far, and soon reached the boundary of the grounds, marked by tall iron railings. The heath stretched away on the other side. Out there, people would be going about their days, unaware of the microcosm she inhabited. She bounced her fingertip along the railings until she met the top of the driveway. The open gates that had welcomed them the night before were closed, and a digital keypad confirmed their desire to keep the world away. Lily pulled her scarf over her hair as the drizzle became rain. Time was up. She picked up her pace, hurrying back, and followed the more direct route of the driveway. The manor was even more impressive in the day. Built from red brick, with tall windows and a flat roof, surrounded by a balustrade. By the majestic front door, two evergreens in square planters stood sentry. She changed course, preferring to circle the house and re-enter via the conservatory. As she passed the bay window of the drawing room, the butler stood stoic in the centre, his hands held behind his slim frame. If he'd spotted her, he didn't let it show. His body was inanimate, his focus fixed, statue-like. Unsettled, Lily tucked her head into her shoulders and scurried past, unsure of whether the grounds were off limits. The instructions hadn't said.

She pulled her scarf from her hair and sheltered in the empty conservatory. No clocks in there, she noted, wondering how long she'd been outside. Someone had tidied the breakfast things away and cleared the tables of crumbs and cutlery. The rhythm of rain tapped on the roof. Lily undid her coat as she slipped through to the hall and back up the wide stairs to put her things in her room. She reached the landing. One of the other doors was ajar. The rooms all had different themes, and she'd yet to see any of the others. Not sure if she should, her curiosity won out. One last furtive look to check if anyone else was around. She edged the door open a little more. She knocked, just in case he was inside, and peeped around the door.

The green room had the feel of a train carriage. Intricate art deco prints lined the walls and met varnished wooden panels. Max's room, the *Orient Express*. She wavered at the boundary, not brave enough to enter, taking in the unmade bed and cluttered nightstand complete with a glass of water and a pill bottle. Maybe Max wasn't as together as he pretended to be. Maybe he was the murderer after all. It was getting difficult to distinguish between what was real and what was part of the story. Not wanting to be discovered, Lily slipped away.

CHAPTER 17

O n the drawing room floor, Jamie rolled his shoulders and stretched. The butler guarded the window, just in case any of the patrons ventured outside and chose an unfortunate time to peer in. The guests had been thorough in their investigations, and muscles he didn't know he had were aching. He rolled onto his back and groaned. He reached his arms high above him, then pushed himself up, tilting his head from side to side, and enjoyed the feeling of movement in his frozen joints. His neck clicked. On the mantelpiece, the carriage clock informed him it was just after ten. He'd been lying still for three hours. Much longer than expected. Jamie had assumed they'd be keen to rush off and continue their inquiries. He'd been wrong. Instead, they'd searched every corner of the drawing room. Lucky he'd locked the door to the attic stairs.

The prosthetic chest under Jamie's shirt ensured the guests couldn't see him breathing, but the stillness of his limbs was all the result of hours of practice and complete concentration. Like the human statues in the city centre – just one pretending to be dead, instead of made from metal for the delight of tourists.

At least the guests had been entertaining. He couldn't see them, but from Grace's first scream until Harvey's last jabbering comment, he'd delighted in all their false turns. A couple of them noticed clues, a couple fell for a red herring, but they didn't know how it all fitted together yet.

Jamie couldn't feel his foot. He circled it and flexed his toes inside the restrictive Oxfords, letting the circulation creep back in, and winced as the numbness became a sharp cramp. He hadn't realised he'd tucked his foot under his leg until Arthur had opened the door. Still, he thought with pride, like a true professional, he'd forced himself through the discomfort, until that too had passed.

The prosthetic had left his skin clammy. He needed a shower, and after all the wine he'd drunk last night, he wouldn't object to a litre of water and maybe some paracetamol. He leaned down and flipped over the rug, hiding the blood stain. Jamie ignored the butler and pressed a panel on the wall to reveal the door concealed behind the bookcase. Inside, a short corridor led to the hallway, another way for the servants of old to move through the house without interrupting the owners and a useful place to hide the white tape he'd stashed there the night before. He passed it to the butler, who knelt to mark the shape of a body on the now clean Oriental rug. Jamie left him to it. He collected the hammer and disappeared up the stairs, pausing mid-flight to make sure the door closed behind him.

In the attic, Jamie sank into the empty chair. He ached all over and rubbed at a knot in his shoulder.

Elliot's pinched face showed his concern. 'You good?'

'Yeah. Won't lie, though. I'm glad that's over. Tell me how things are coming along.'

They both turned their attention to the large monitors on the walls, the familiar carousel of rooms. Elliot passed Jamie a bag of salt and vinegar crisps.

'Breakfast of champions,' Jamie said. They grinned like small boys getting up to mischief. Jamie's stomach grumbled as he tore open the bag, letting him know he'd need to eat something more substantial than crisps at some point.

He rubbed the back of his neck and rolled his shoulders. Elliot unscrewed the top of a bottle of water by his feet and ripped the corner off a paper packet of re-hydration remedy. He concentrated as he tipped the purple powder into the top of the bottle and swirled it around as it fizzed.

Jamie accepted the bottle from Elliot, took a swig, and grimaced. 'What's next?' he asked. 'And why do they make this stuff so foul?'

Elliot laughed as Jamie drank it all down, even the grainy bits at the bottom. 'Punishment for overindulgence.' Elliot pushed his glasses up his nose. 'Okay, here's where we are. We've got Grace and Arthur in the library. Carol, Harvey and Debbie are in the billiard room. Lily's just come back from a walk around the grounds, and Kevin's on his own in his bedroom. Getting dressed, I hope. Those pyjamas were revolting.'

'I heard,' Jamie said. 'One advantage of having my eyes closed.'

The butler ambled around the drawing room, making a last check of the changes that transformed it from a murder scene to a crime scene. He inspected each piece of furniture, each ornament, then spun around and stared up at one of the hidden cameras.

'That man gives me the creeps.' Elliot shuddered. 'I don't know where you found him, but let's hire someone different next time. What does he think he's doing?' He gripped the arms of the chair. 'It would be a disaster if the guests saw him doing that.'

He had a point, but there was nothing to be gained by getting rattled, and Jamie chose not to mention that Elliot had done the same thing earlier.

'It's fine,' Jamie said. 'He's just letting us know he's done and the room can be used again. I'll have a quiet word later, when the cocktails are being served.'

'Thanks. I'd appreciate it.' Elliot's shoulders dropped. He'd always hated confrontation. 'As long as none of the guests think it's him. Can you imagine what it would be like if we made it all the way to the big reveal dinner, and the guests thought the butler did it?'

A pigeon landed on the windowsill and cooed, using the height of the building to view the world beneath. There was plenty of time for the guests to work through the clues, to consider their conclusions and to prepare for the eight-course feast planned for that evening. Soon they'd know who'd accuse who, and whether their chosen murderer would avoid detection.

Jamie kicked off the Oxfords without untying them and wiggled his toes again. He crossed his feet at the ankles and leaned back in the chair. He watched the screens and tried to focus. His head grew heavy and fell to the side. He sensed the comforting weight of a blanket and half-heard Elliot leave the room in favour of being front of house again. Returning to his role as eccentric host. As Jamie drifted into that space between awake and asleep; he dreamed, and his dreams were filled with murder.

He woke with a jolt, disorientated, worried he was still in the drawing room. He squinted at the digital clock in the corner of one screen and saw he'd been asleep for nearly two hours. Carol and Harvey caught his attention, huddled together in the hall. He rubbed his neck and followed their progress as they tiptoed up the stairs like a pair of comedy robbers. Reaching the first floor, they dashed to Kevin's room and brazenly opened the door he hadn't thought to lock. Brilliant. While Elliot was busy schmoozing, Jamie could watch the action unfold from the comfort of his chair. His muscles still ached from hours of playing dead, but now he felt invigorated. This was fun.

Harvey peeked inside Kevin's room. Jamie had to admit it was one of his favourites. Instead of focusing on a particular novel like he had for the others, he'd filled this one with detective paraphernalia dedicated to a single character. Deep maroon walls enclosed dark mahogany furniture and details scattered about, from the magnifying glass left as if by accident on the bedside table, through to the tweed bedspread.

Harvey stepped inside, with Carol following like a shadow. She didn't bother to close the door behind her, giving Jamie a decent view of their snooping from the camera in the hall. There was a delicious irony in them not knowing he could see them. He zoomed in.

The room was a complete mess. Clothes spilled out of Kevin's suitcase, left open in the middle of the floor. He'd not even bothered to hang up his jacket from dinner and had left it crumpled in the corner. There was a discarded coffee cup on the windowsill, the bed was unmade, and a pile of old newspapers had been stacked on the elegant writing table.

'How odd.' Harvey stopped by the stack. 'Who brings their old newspapers with them on a weekend away? They're all open at the crossword, and I wouldn't say our man Kevin is much of a wordsmith. Most of them are incomplete.'

Carol swallowed hard and continued her own inspection, peering over without touching anything. Harvey determined to make a more thorough search and picked up items with the careful fingertips of one concerned they might catch something.

'This is so naughty.' Carol's face flushed with delight. 'I'm not sure there's anything here that implicates he's the murderer, though.'

'No, I agree. He's certainly not going to win any prizes for tidiness anytime soon, but you're right, nothing smacks of guilt.'

The clock in the hall chimed, and they froze mid-search like they'd set off a burglar alarm.

'Our cue to give up, I think,' Harvey said. Carol edged towards the door while he took a final half-hearted look and lifted the stack of newspapers. 'Hold on a minute, there's a writing pad here, with a list of all our names printed on it.'

Carol peered around him. 'That's nothing, surely. I've made notes about the others, and I'm sure you have too.'

'No, I mean, yes, I have. But that's not what's strange. Apart from this being the only neat thing in the room, Kevin's written his own name, and there's a red line through it.'

'That doesn't make sense.' Carol screwed up her face. 'If it's a list of suspects, why would he write his own name?'

Harvey rubbed his face. 'Let's consider the tropes. He could have just written the names of all the suspects, included himself, and then crossed his name off. The murderer could have planted it, or it could be a red herring.'

'Not very helpful.'

'No. Even so, I still think it's him.'

'Me too.' Carol started searching again.

'I wonder what his wife's like,' Harvey said. 'I wonder if the poor woman spends her time tidying up after him, or whether she's as bad as he is. Can you imagine two of them, swaying through life, being that disagreeable? Doesn't bear thinking about.' He shivered. Carol knelt on the floor to search under the bed. From Jamie's viewpoint, all he could see was her behind sticking up in the air.

'Sorry, I didn't catch that.' She re-emerged, her hair ruffled from the bedspread. She patted her bob back into place.

'Never mind,' Harvey said. 'Let's rescue Debbie and maybe get some lunch. All this investigation is making me hungry.'

'Let's.'

In the attic, Jamie reclined in the chair. It was all coming together, just as they'd planned.

CHAPTER 18

D ebbie searched for Kevin. She wanted to speak to him alone. Well, 'wanted to' might be a tad strong, but after she'd sent Carol and Harvey off to do some snooping, she decided it would be prudent to keep him busy. She found him in the billiard room. He'd changed out of those awful tartan pyjamas, although the tanned corduroy trousers and beige shirt weren't much of an upgrade. One trouser leg was longer than the other. A stray thread trailed behind him. He likely thought no one would notice. Debbie had. She imagined him at home demanding that 'the wife', as he referred to her, fix them, and her stopping whatever else she was doing to pander to his needs. How some women lived like that, she just couldn't fathom.

She held back to observe. He stroked the smooth edge of the billiard table before she approached, careful to keep an appropriate distance from this repulsive little man.

She fixed her polite, work smile on her face and asked, 'Do you play?' She gestured towards the table, surprised when he engaged.

'Used to play snooker at the local club before it closed down. I always thought billiards was for toffs who weren't rich enough for a full-sized table at home and too stuck-up to play with the rest of us.'

He didn't even have the courtesy of looking at her while he talked to her. Infuriating. She hated when people did that.

Still, she persevered. 'They're rich enough for a games room in the first place. That's more than most of us.'

Debbie actually was affluent enough to have a games room if she chose. She could quite easily afford to buy a property with such amenities. That she could, and had decided not to, was a level of detail she had no intention of getting into with Kevin. She reminded herself this was not the time to start an argument. She was here with a purpose and must remain focused.

'Were you any good?' Most men, she found, relished the chance to share their sporting prowess. It never ceased to amaze her how many of them had been destined for careers as professional footballers until injury scuppered their ambitions.

'Not particularly,' he said, with surprising honesty. 'Never had enough spare time to practise, too busy at work. Not that we can play now, we only have the black.' He pointed to a solitary billiard ball nestled by the pocket in the far corner, then bent to see if the other balls hid in the rack beneath. He huffed, empty-handed.

While Kevin continued his search for equipment, Debbie patrolled the room, as if she'd intended to do that all along, and his presence was a complete coincidence. Like most of the rooms in this large Georgian house, the fireplace was the focal point. The billiard table itself was lengthwise to the window, where a large leather sofa waited for spectators. By the edge of the fireplace, a deck of cards sat on a table covered in green fabric. The eight of spades faced upwards. Kevin picked up the card and rolled it over his knuckles as if he was practising a magic trick. 'Maybe it's a clue.'

'Yes, maybe.' Her tone deliberately implied this was ridiculous, although she suspected he might be right. He carried a sort of forlorn air about him, like someone who'd walked into something they didn't comprehend and couldn't work out how to get away again.

'Oh, I don't know,' he said. 'Maybe I should have just stayed at home and enjoyed having the house to myself while the wife is away.'

Debbie gave a mock-sympathetic nod, attempting to hide her loathing for self-pity. This interview was shaping up as an admission of melancholy, rather than murder.

'I could have enjoyed doing all the things I'm never normally allowed to do. You've all teamed up, and I'm on my own anyway.' He dropped the card and bent to retrieve it.

'Nonsense,' Debbie said. 'I'm not in a team. I'm here with you.'

He was right again, though. The others had all formed alliances of sorts, and no one had invited him to join them. Human nature dictated you surround yourself with people either like you or who contributed skills you lacked. So, while she wouldn't say Carol or Harvey were her most natural allies, Harvey's gift for recognising the key mystery tropes was narrowing the field, and Carol's maternal charm encouraged people to talk. Debbie had selected them for her unofficial team on purpose. Kevin, however, was not like any of the others and didn't bring valuable skills. In another life, she might have felt sorry for him. There was a fine line between pity and irritation.

What Kevin didn't know – and why would he? – was that Debbie's cohort had devised a strategy earlier, one they were currently implementing. They'd decided Kevin needed to be interviewed, and she'd volunteered to find out whether he might be the murderer. Neither Carol nor Harvey had been brave enough to speak to him, and she was the most used to dealing with difficult personalities as part of her job. She just needed to work out which triggers worked with him and, sadly, the only way to do that was through conversation. The billiard discussion hadn't worked, so she tried something more generic.

'How are you finding the manor?'

Kevin chewed his lip. 'It's nice enough. The room's a bit on the small side and the wine was a tad disappointing.'

She struggled to believe that after how much he'd drunk the night before. And by the way he dressed, she very much doubted he was used to living the life of luxury. Not that you could always judge people by your first impressions.

Every now and again, someone came along who caught you off guard. Kevin, though, struck her as one of those people who was never content, no matter what blessings came their way. She wondered if he'd always been like that, or if it was a learned behaviour.

Then he let slip something of interest. 'I'm not allowed to drink wine at home.'

'Really?'

'The wife.' A simple statement of fact. Bitter and miserable.

'Ah,' she said, understanding. 'It must be hard to balance the things you like with those that are good for you.'

'I suppose.'

Kevin returned the card, face up on the deck. The eight of spades, symbol of life's sorrows. She wasn't sure how she knew that. As well as his generic unpleasantness, 'sorrowful' described Kevin perfectly. This wasn't the time for pity. There were more pressing matters, namely that of whether he'd committed Jamie's murder. He, like most of the other guests, claimed to have been in his themed room asleep when the deed took place. They'd all had the opportunity, assuming Harvey hadn't done it as the last to see Jamie alive. No. Too obvious.

The second question Debbie pondered was one of motive, and that was harder to confirm. Just because Kevin was irksome, didn't necessarily mean he was a murderer, and his lack of affability could be part of the character created for the game. She just couldn't be sure. Debbie moved to the top of the billiard table and maintained her own character, pretending she was interested, and continuing to prompt. She hoped Carol and Harvey had found something, and that they'd be back to relieve her soon.

In the meantime, she persevered. 'What line of work are you in?'

They'd touched on the subject the night before. She waited for his reply. She always told the staff they were blessed with 'two ears and one mouth' and that should be the listening to speaking ratio.

He rewarded her patience. 'Property,' he said. 'Local lettings.'

Now, that was interesting.

'Fascinating. I'd love to know your thoughts on the development of this property.' She wanted him to believe she valued his opinion.

He took the bait.

'It's different here to my local patch,' he said. 'This house is Georgian, obviously. About average size for the time. We say "manor" these days and assume airs and graces, but these detached homes were pretty standard in their day. Round my way, developers have bought and carved up anything this size into flats and sold them off one by one. If this one hit the open market, they'd probably build back into the garden to maximise the profit. I'd guess the boys soon found a pretty substantial renovation project on their hands. There's no way a top spec property like this would be anywhere near affordable to convert into a game.'

Debbie inspected the grand space. 'I wonder how they afforded it.' Not that she expected Kevin to know. 'I'm sure they said they'd been travelling and then got menial jobs. Even in a rundown state, this type of project must have cost an absolute fortune.'

'Yes, it would. I found a letter in my room giving some background about the property. From what it said, Elliot inherited the manor, but you're right, the building work would still have cost tens of thousands at least.'

It niggled her. How Jamie and Elliot found the money to create the game. There could be an investment opportunity here somewhere. She'd be keen to explore that. Not her current focus though, so she filed the idea away to give more thought to later. Time to offer Kevin a little flattery and see if she could find out any more.

'You know your stuff,' she said. 'What can you tell me about the layout? Is that in keeping with the style of the day?'

Kevin nodded. He gave the impression he knew what he was talking about for once. How unexpected. It appeared the one thing he liked in life was his job. They had something in common, after all.

'I'd say so. There are a lot of original features, these fireplaces and the floor tiles in the hallway, for example. I'd guess the servants' quarters are still intact and there would have been a whole maze of hidden passages and staircases to let them do their work without disturbing the family. A lot of developers knocked into the staircases when they converted to flats, or they used them to create maisonettes. It's unusual to find one intact.'

Curious indeed. Hidden passages might be far-fetched, but it would help their hosts orchestrate the game without being seen. On the flip side, just because Kevin knew of their existence didn't make him the guilty party. It's not like he'd withheld the information.

Carol and Harvey bundled in. Carol giggled. Debbie gave her a reproachful stare, warning her to get a hold of herself. They'd taken longer upstairs than they'd agreed. Debbie would speak to them about that later.

Kevin pursed his lips. 'Taking it all seriously, then?'

Harvey crossed the room. Debbie thought for a moment he was about to confront Kevin. Instead, he moved past and lowered himself into an armchair. 'Mother always said, the best mysteries fill you with fear and joy in equal measure. It's not real life, Kevin. It's entertainment.'

'What was she like?' Debbie said. 'If you don't mind me asking. She must have had an astonishing career, and I'd love to know more.'

'That, she did.'

Debbie settled in the armchair across from him. She folded her hands on her lap.

Harvey told his story. 'Mother was formidable. The famous Mary Bakewell, who didn't allow for excuses and insisted anything was possible. She had a hard life, don't get me wrong. A life filled with knocks as well as brilliant success. There are some things she always refused to speak of, even to me. I've got a fair bit of time to myself when she's asleep or watching television, so I've done some research. I quite like the idea of writing her biography. I think it would be a fitting tribute when she's...'

'What a lovely idea.' Carol took his hand, interrupting him, so he didn't need to say the words. 'What have you found out so far?'

'Well,' he said. 'She began writing to make some money when she fell pregnant with me.'

'What about your father?'

Kevin, always first with the inappropriate comment.

'No. He wasn't on the scene. I've never been able to track him down, but from what I gather from Mum's diaries, he was an older man, possibly her employer.'

'How awful.' Carol patted her hair.

However, it impressed Debbie. 'She was brave to keep a baby in those days.'

There was still a way to go, but women's rights had improved considerably since the time of Harvey's birth, and she held a deep respect for those who refused to adhere to the rules laid down by men. Harvey's eyes were damp. This story wasn't made up for the weekend. This was true.

'Mother was always so courageous.' He rubbed the side of his face. 'Still is. She told me about the day she wrote her first ever chapter. She swung open the window in her rented room and let the birdsong in. The world went by beneath and she watched, amazed the people passing were so unaware of her just above them. She marvelled at their individuality and their spirit, but most of all, she was interested in their secrets. She pondered whether everyone concealed a hidden agenda, a dream, or personal drama. She supposed they must.'

'Just like here.' Carol interrupted again. Debbie took a sharp breath in.

Harvey didn't seem to mind. 'I dare say. Mother insists she didn't know what she was doing when she settled down at the desk overlooking that road and made notes about the people. She stayed there all day, in her nightgown, combining characteristics, turns of phrase and mannerisms, until she created eight fully formed characters ready to embark on a story of her making.'

Debbie leaned forwards. 'Eight characters. You said there were eight?'

'Hmm, yes, apparently there's some psychology or other that says the perfect number of suspects in a mystery is eight. It's something to do with the brain's ability to process clues. Makes it almost impossible for the reader to work out who did it until it's all disclosed at the end.'

'Fascinating.' Harvey was full of surprises.

'Yes. Obviously, Mum didn't know that then. Just some sort of author intuition. She told me she'd write all day. She wrote longhand, until her hands were so stiff, she could barely hold the pen. I've still got some of those early notes in a box in the loft. You can tell the start and end of a session by the handwriting.

'She tried to teach herself to write with the other hand, but never got the hang of it. She made sure I learned when I was a child. I had a lot of fun tricking the teachers.'

'How wonderful.' Carol clapped. 'Please carry on.'

'After that, she took all her savings and bought a second-hand typewriter. She spent the next six months typing out her words before dawn woke the rest of the city. When she arrived home from work, she'd go straight back to it. When she couldn't hide her pregnancy anymore, she moved, dressed in black, and told her new neighbours she'd been widowed. They were good people. Never complained about the constant clack of the typewriter and never questioned the story she'd given them, although they probably guessed the truth. She sent her first manuscript out, and that was it, the dawn of her illustrious career.'

'What was it like for you growing up like that?' Carol asked.

'The rhythmic sound of typing was the music of my childhood. Mum would read out her first draft, making corrections as she went, and then, when I was old enough to read, she appointed me her proofreader. It was a happy life, quiet, simple. We spent a lot of time together in those fictional worlds. Then Mum became quite famous, and didn't need me so much. I moved out and got a proper job.'

'And what did you do?' Debbie didn't miss a beat. Maybe Harvey's job would provide further insight, in the same way as Kevin's had.

'I'd always loved cars and my teachers always said I was pretty good at talking, so I worked at the local car dealership.'

'She must be very proud,' Carol said. 'She'll enjoy hearing all about the weekend, I'm sure.'

Kevin gave a snort. 'Multiple times.'

No one else appreciated the comment.

Debbie's head snapped around to address him and put him back in his place. She caught herself and challenged instead. 'If you're so wise, who do you think the murderer is?'

Kevin gave a sly smile. 'I'm surprised you don't know. I think it's pretty obvious.' Abhorrent little man.

CHAPTER 19

Muffled voices came from the billiard room, and as it was the only communal area Lily had yet to investigate, she decided to do just that. Like the rest of the house, it was comfortable and lavish. Interiors just weren't like this anymore, in an age of spotlights and neutral shades. Even her mother's house, where she'd resisted modern designs, because 'there's nothing wrong' with how they'd decorated the family home a decade ago, appeared busy and cluttered, rather than comforting in the way this place was. The manor had captivated Lily from the moment she'd walked through the door, from the ornaments to the dark wooden furniture, and even intricacies in the patterns in the wallpaper, that may or may not be clues.

Harvey reclined in an armchair by the fireplace. His hands rested on his tummy, with Debbie opposite, like she'd been interrogating him. Carol and Kevin were there too, at either end of the mantelpiece. Carol's hair appeared lopsided, slipped to one side. She patted it, adjusting it back into place. It didn't shock Lily to realise it was a wig, but she couldn't help being annoyed at herself for not noticing sooner. Now she thought about it, the haircut didn't suit its wearer. Lily hadn't even considered it, preferring to judge people on who they are instead of what they look like, and wishing others did the same. She wondered if any of the others had noticed, and whether it was a clue. The wooden clock in the corner chimed, giving a natural break to whatever debate they'd been involved in.

'Ah, hello again, Lily,' Harvey said. 'How was your walk?'

She considered what she should share, whether to mention the bizarre butler who'd stood in the window as she'd passed. Elliot made the decision for her as he swept in with his normal flourish. He always seemed to know the precise moment to let his presence be known. He wore his black three-piece suit and a wide smile.

'Good afternoon.' He spoke to them all, but smiled in her direction. 'I trust your investigations are progressing to your satisfaction. Lunch is ready in the conservatory if anyone's peckish, and there'll be afternoon tea at four in the library.'

'Perfect timing.' Harvey patted his knees and rocked to get up from the armchair.

So much food. Lily didn't think she could manage lunch, afternoon tea, and a multiple-course dinner.

Elliot checked his pocket watch. 'None of it's compulsory, of course. If you plan to choose one or the other, I'd hold out for tea. The freshly baked scones are delicious, and it's rather a quaint custom.'

'Oh, I think we can squeeze them both in.' Harvey offered his arm to Carol. 'Shall we?'

'Absolutely.' She looped her arm through his with a giggle. 'It would be rude not to.'

'I'll join you if you don't mind,' Debbie said, doing a poor job of pretending they weren't going off to compare notes.

'Delighted.'

The unlikely trio wandered off to the conservatory in search of lunch, leaving Kevin alone like a solitary bookend.

Elliot chose a place at the card table. 'Fancy a game?' He collected the cards together and shuffled them. The fire warmed Lily's side. Elliot dealt, and she spread a card fan in front of her face.

Max passed by the open door. Lily gave him a finger wave and played her first card. Kevin's stance stiffened as Max approached. In any other context, Lily told herself, she wouldn't eavesdrop. Normal rules didn't apply in a murder mystery, though, and anyway, she really wanted to hear what they had to say.

'Hey,' Max said, and the awkward silence of two people with nothing in common hung in the air. Elliot laid a card on the table and waited for Lily to take her turn.

Max persevered with Kevin. 'Did you explore the gardens before the rain set in? The rose garden must be beautiful in the summer.'

Lily slipped a card from the middle of her fan, still pretending she wasn't listening to the stilted conference on the other side of the room.

'No,' Kevin said. 'I've roses at home. I know what they look like.'

Dismissive and rude. But if Max intended to try again, he wouldn't get the opportunity.

Kevin manoeuvred around the billiard table, flustered. 'I think I'll get some lunch as well.'

He knocked Lily's shoulder as he passed without apology.

'Well, that went well,' she said. 'Come and watch me win at cards.' Lily laid her last card, and Elliot gave her a brief round of applause.

'Bravo,' he said, 'game to you. I'm afraid duty calls. I'll leave you to it for now and let you conclude your investigations, unless there's anything you need.'

She might be wrong, but she thought he wanted her to need something, and she'd have liked him to stay. She'd never admit it, though, and he must be busy. She didn't want to be a bother.

'No. I'm fine. Thank you.'

Elliot stood and bowed.

Max slipped into Elliot's place. 'Go on, then. Let's see these card-shark skills in action.' Rain lashed against the bay window. Behind it, the dark, ominous sky. The forecast had been right. Lily tapped the cards together and rested them in a neat pile on the green fabric. She adjusted them until they lined up perfectly against the edge.

For the second time that day, Arthur and Grace found her and Max together. Arthur entered the room first, no doubt keen to make sure that no unexpected bodies lay behind the door this time.

Grace slid past and gave Lily a warm smile as she claimed the free space. 'Hello, dear,' she said. 'How have you been getting along?'

Lily couldn't tell if she meant with Max or with the murder, and didn't ask.

Arthur stood behind Grace, his hand on the back of her chair. He made a show of checking his watch. 'We've plenty of time for a few rounds before afternoon tea.'

'Good idea,' Grace said.

'I'll warn you,' Max said. 'She's got skills.'

'I'll take that as a compliment.' Lily grinned and dealt the cards.

Max bounced the unanswered question back to the couple. 'And how have *you* been getting on?'

'Famously.' Grace contemplated her cards. 'Arthur worked out the clues pretty early on, so we've spent most of the morning seeing how many we could find and making sure we have a robust case. It's been thrilling to explore the manor, such an impressive building, and we even managed a quick tour of the grounds before all this rain set in.' She waved her hand at the window as if to shoo the rain away. 'What I'd really like to do is get behind scenes and explore all those secret passages.'

Lily studied the wall. 'I know what you mean. I wonder if they'll show us around after the murderer is revealed. It would be terrific material for my novel.' She glanced at the floor, not sure if she'd shared too much, wishing she hadn't spoken.

'Oh, a writer. How marvellous,' Grace said. 'I'd love to read your work when you're ready. When we collect our phones tomorrow, I'll find you on social media and we can keep in touch.'

Max played his card. 'You sound like the kids at the centre, always on their phones.'

Lily could imagine Grace as a silver surfer. Arthur coughed and selected his card. Max shifted in his chair. There was a clap of thunder and the lights wavered.

CHAPTER 20

T he screens in the control room flickered and went off, the dark surfaces reflecting distorted images of Jamie and Elliot back at themselves. Jamie needed those screens functioning. Without them, he'd be working blind. Not ideal.

'The storm's picking up,' Elliot said. Ever one to state the obvious.

'Do you think?' He tried to keep the irritation out of his voice as he took the laptop from Elliot. Another low rumble of thunder shook the manor. The attic was not the most relaxing place to be in a storm.

The standby light on the main screen came back on as the screens reset, and Jamie meticulously checked each room as it came back online. 'I think we're okay, just a short, seems to be working again. Sorry I snapped. Right, let's take a look at what they're all up to.'

Debbie, Harvey and Carol persevered with lunch in the conservatory while rain pelted the glass ceiling. A fork of lightning split the sky and changed their minds.

Debbie picked up her plate. 'I suggest we relocate. Personally, I'd prefer to enjoy my meal under a more solid structure.'

'No arguments here.' Carol pushed back from the table.

Harvey put his knife and fork together on his plate. 'Me either.'

Jamie switched cameras and followed them through the hall. Their motley procession in search of shelter from the storm. Debbie led them to the drawing room and the three of them positioned themselves on the sofas around the Oriental rug, balancing their plates on their laps.

Carol's knife slipped as she cut a piece of ham. She picked up the slice, rolled it and popped it whole into her mouth. 'It's like nothing ever happened,' she said. 'I wonder where Jamie is now.'

In the attic, Jamie waved at the screen. Now they were back online he could enjoy himself again. Elliot peered over his glasses at him, a tad unsettled still. At least he'd calmed down now the screens were back. Downstairs, Debbie kept her group focused on the task at hand, just as she always did. She was as relentless as Jamie expected her to be.

'It's not important where Jamie is,' she said. 'What's important is what you found in Kevin's room.'

Harvey put his empty plate on the floor and tucked it under the chair. 'He's a messy chap, for sure.' He rested his hands on his stomach. 'He's brought a pile of old newspapers with him for some reason, and he'd written a list of all the guests with his name crossed off. Odd, but nothing conclusive. Did you do any better when you spoke to him?'

'I did actually.' Debbie twisted a piece of hair around her finger. 'It transpires Kevin is an estate agent, of all things, and is considerably more knowledgeable than you'd expect. He told me these old manor houses were riddled with secret passages.'

'Interesting.' Harvey rubbed the side of his face. 'We could go searching.'

'I'm not cheating,' Carol said.

Debbie rolled her eyes. 'You've literally just been snooping around Kevin's room. And anyway, they didn't give us any rules about the servants' quarters, so I don't see why we can't.' She put her plate on the low coffee table. 'It's decided, then. Let's explore some more before afternoon tea.'

'That's so naughty,' Carol said.

In the attic, Elliot pushed himself up. 'So much for a few hours' rest. I guess that's me checking we've locked all the doors to the servants' areas.'

Jamie considered. 'We could just leave them. There's only a couple of hours until afternoon tea, and like they said, they've already snooped around each other's rooms. What difference will it make?'

Elliot stayed unconvinced. 'What if they find you? You're meant to be dead.'

'Okay, you distract them. Maybe mention you know someone searched Kevin's room. Drop a hint that behind scenes are off limits. Maybe even promise them a tour in the morning once the reveal is done. I'll keep watch from up here and make sure I stay hidden.'

'I suppose.'

Jamie pressed the point. 'It's not like there's anything up here we'd mind if they saw.'

Elliot checked his pocket watch, then caught himself. No need to do that when he was behind the scenes. 'Sure. I guess I'll do that, then. We're so close, it would be a pity to ruin it all now.'

'Good man. All agreed. It'll be fine.'

A flash of lightning startled Jamie, but now was not the time to leave his post. Seconds later, Elliot materialised in the drawing room and distracted the adventuring trio by stacking the empty plates they'd discarded. Even if he didn't think so himself, Elliot was rather skilled at this. Debbie tapped her foot while Elliot drew Harvey into another storytelling session, something about vintage cars that Jamie lost interest in.

He switched cameras. Grace and Arthur were halfway up the stairs. Arthur gripped the banister as he inched forwards. Grace supported his other side. They reached the landing and disappeared into their room, leaving nothing of interest to see. He switched again, checked the billiard room and confirmed Lily and Max were still playing cards. A low rumble of thunder.

Ideally, they would keep the guests away from the servants' quarters. Still, if they pried this far up, so be it. They'd manage. He checked the time – not long until the big reveal. He watched the screens and tapped his foot. The storm raged on.

CHAPTER 21

Debbie couldn't remember the last time she'd partaken of afternoon tea. As Elliot had rightly said, it was such a quaint custom, and one she'd enjoy observing some of the more determinedly masculine staff on her team taking part in. Rows of leather-bound books lined the shelves behind her. She inspected the contents of a three-tier stand, ladened with sandwiches, cakes and scones. Blue-glazed bone china cups and saucers nestled next to delicate plates. The setup was charming.

Debbie detected movement in the hall, and while she waited for the others to arrive, she reflected on the excellent work she'd conducted that day. She slipped her feet out of her high heels and wriggled the circulation back into her toes. She should probably invest in some sensible shoes like the ones Lily wore. Like that was ever going to happen. Still, apart from her aching toes, Debbie felt energised. She hadn't answered an email, written a report or spoken to a client for coming up on twenty-four hours and she couldn't remember the last time she'd done that. She used to wonder what people did at the weekend when they weren't working. It surprised her to find it a pleasant experience. Maybe she should find a hobby. She'd ask Milly to research one for her on Monday.

The others were pleasant enough, with their comforting chatter. More importantly, the weekend was providing her the head space to think about her life and what she wanted to do with it. She wanted to win first, because, well, winning was what she did, and she had a pretty solid idea of who the killer was. Not that it mattered, it's not like it was an actual crime. What mattered more was whether she wanted to go back to her immaculate house where she lived alone, and her important job, where she felt alone. There had to be more to life.

Harvey interrupted her thoughts. In another context, this would have irritated her, but, she realised with surprise, she'd grown fond of him.

'Anything more to report?' She'd left him talking about cars with Elliot a few hours ago. Making her excuses to finalise her case.

'Not really.'

He picked up a cucumber sandwich and took a bite. Debbie hoped he wasn't holding out on her. It would be most disappointing to find out her makeshift team had failed to mention vital information just hours before they committed to their conclusions. Before she could quiz him further, Lily tiptoed in. Such a timid little creature.

Debbie waved at the free chair to her side. 'Do come and join us.'

Lily did as she was told.

The butler hovered in the hallway. She wished he'd just decide whether to be in the room or outside of it. There was still something about him that didn't fit. He was always there, lurking in the background, and while she couldn't fault his attention to detail, he made her uncomfortable. Nothing made Debbie uncomfortable. A most unsettling feeling.

Grace joined their party. No Arthur, for some reason. Grace unfolded a napkin and settled it on her lap.

'What have you done with that husband of yours?' Debbie asked.

'He's just having a bit of a rest. All this excitement can get tiring at our age.'

'Well, we're pleased you could join us.' Debbie suspected he was off somewhere searching for clues. They'd been confident they had the mystery pinned down earlier. Not that confidence meant anything in this particular situation. It seemed it would just be the four of them for afternoon tea. The butler graced them with his presence, emerging from the shadows in the hall to pour the tea. Earl grey.

Lily added a dash of milk. 'My favourite.'

The soft flames of the fire crackled behind the iron grate as the storm rumbled on in the background. The butler finished pouring the tea, then took a long metal pole from behind the curtains and used it to pull the velvet drapes across the window. Debbie was glad she wasn't battling to get to a client meeting in this. Harvey selected a scone and cut it in half, then lathered it with strawberry jam from a ramekin. He used a different knife to add clotted cream.

Grace picked up a knife. 'I can never remember if it's Cornwall or Devon that put the jam on first.'

'I think it's Cornwall.' Harvey covered his full mouth with his hand. 'Elliot was telling the truth. These are delicious. Try one.'

Debbie took a plain scone. She'd never been keen on raisins.

Lily did the same. 'Let's make one of each, and we can compare.'

She prepared one half of her scone with jam and cream, the other, the other way round. All very civilised. The four didn't say a great deal. Whether people were keeping their clues close to their chests was hard to tell. Debbie relaxed into her chair and sipped her tea.

'Hello,' Elliot said. Why he always felt the need to announce himself when he entered a room was beyond her. He blushed as he beamed at Lily. The poor girl hadn't realised he'd developed a crush yet. Or identified her own feelings, for that matter. Debbie might give them a little nudge at some point if she felt so inclined.

'Hello, dear,' Grace said. 'You were right. The scones are wonderful. And this library, it must have taken generations to collect all these volumes?'

Elliot checked his pocket watch. 'Dinner will be served at 8pm.' He'd ignored her question and provided yet another unnecessary instruction, like he was working from a script, which, she supposed, was feasible. Still, they'd all read the itinerary and there was plenty of time to get ready.

'Yes, we know,' Debbie said. 'Come and tell us a bit more about how you and Jamie came up with the concept for the weekend. I'm sure we'd all like to know.'

'Poor Jamie.' Harvey picked up another sandwich and took a bite.

'He's not really dead,' Grace said.

Harvey lowered his gaze and finished chewing before he spoke. 'I know.'

'Well, I can't give too much away,' Elliot said. 'But I can tell you it's been a lifelong dream of ours to go into business together.'

'How long have you known each other?' Debbie fiddled with her napkin, pretending this was just a passing interest.

'Since we were children,' he said. 'Jamie joined my school when we were about eight and we've been friends ever since.'

'How sweet.' Grace sipped her tea. 'And how did you afford this house, if that's not a secret part of the game?'

'I inherited it. We borrowed some money from the bank and my parents helped. The rest is all blood, sweat, and tears.'

His accent slipped slightly and Debbie considered whether his diction was a clue.

'That's brave.' Lily didn't look at him when she spoke; she so rarely did.

'Well, Jamie's always been excellent at making ideas a reality.' Elliot took a bite of a smoked salmon sandwich and changed the subject. 'Anyway, if you'd care to join us for an aperitif before dinner, we'll collect your summations ahead of the big reveal.'

He was so theatrical, in his tweed, with the chain of his silver pocket watch to the side, and that wonderful BBC accent. All part of the costume, she supposed, and all part of the show. Debbie could tell there was more to his story. More than he was willing to share. Jamie must be the driving force. She'd liaise with him tomorrow, assuming he'd miraculously come back to life after they'd announced the murderer. There were a few adaptations she'd like to make when she brought the team to the manor and saw no reason he wouldn't be open to her suggestions. She'd make it worth his while.

Grace patted the corner of her mouth. 'I think I'd better go and wake Arthur.'

Harvey rose and offered her his hand to help her up. 'Let me escort you.'

'Thank you, dear. How kind.'

'I'll head up too,' Lily said.

Debbie wasn't sure what all the rush was about. There was plenty of time. She padded barefoot over to the bookshelves and browsed the titles. Leather-bound classics, gold embossed. She chose one at random and flipped the pages without reading a word. Instead, she pondered the guests, the manor, the murder. The butler emerged once more from the shadows and gathered up the empty cups. She ignored him.

CHAPTER 22

L ily drifted around her room. She imagined herself in a floating gown, lady of the manor, and enjoyed some quiet time to decompress after being with the others for so long. All that peopling, she just wasn't used to it. Debbie seemed to find it so natural, and Lily wondered how she did it. The woman was a powerhouse. Lily stood at the window and reviewed her character sheets. Rain dashed against the other side.

She wondered what Elliot was like in real life. She liked his host persona, a character with pure diction and polish, even if there were little things in his posture and the way he spoke that gave away it wasn't quite natural for him. The accent was ridiculous, all his words exaggerated, enunciated with the precision of an old-fashioned radio presenter. It couldn't be what he sounded like normally.

She imagined him in front of a mirror, contorting his face to make the sounds, and settled at the dressing table to do the same.

She formed her lips into a perfect 'o' as she said, 'Good afternooon, it's soo nice to meet yooou.'

It was a lot more difficult than she'd expected.

Lily held her breath as she slipped her glittering emerald gown over her head, then swung from side to side as the tassels danced. She admired the result in the mirror once more. She knew she'd never be conventionally pretty. She'd always consoled herself that plain people went unnoticed most of the time, and most of the time, that's what she wanted. Just not all the time.

She'd only been able to afford one evening dress for the two dinners, and she worried she'd made a mistake. The invitation hadn't specified multiple costumes and Elliot wore the same outfit as yesterday, so she hoped it would be okay. Too late now. It would have to be.

With dinner fast approaching, she needed to decide who she'd accuse. She sat with one stockinged foot tucked under her and reviewed the notes taped up against the dark night. The clues clearly suggested the guilty party was Kevin. Horrible man. Lily rarely disliked anyone. She preferred to focus on the good in people, but it was like he was doing everything possible to alienate the others. So, clues and character equalled guilt. And if it was him, maybe he'd shed the character bit once he'd been exposed and turn out to be a nice person. Fingers crossed.

Accusation decided, she settled at the dressing table and edged forwards until she was close to the mirror's surface, almost close enough to fall through into the world on the other side. If she'd thought proper elocution required strange facial expressions, the application of eyeliner came a close second. Her sister had taught her how to do this when she was still in primary school, too young really. In the days before online tutorials, having an older sister to show you these things was a valuable commodity, and having a popular older sister when you were clumsy and quiet was both a blessing and a curse.

Lily never took her for granted, even if she didn't always agree with the advice that was thrust upon her. Her mother encouraged her to be more like her sister; insisting that pretty and popular were a gateway to marriage. It was a mould that Lily didn't fit into and she soon gave up pretending she did. She tried hard not to let a touch of resentment creep in, even now. It took a lot of effort to stay true to what she wanted to do and not what others wanted from her.

Max understood. In a series of strange coincidences, they had that in common too. Both got energy from their creative pursuits, both were searching to find their way through life. The pills she'd spotted in his room troubled her, and she wanted to ask him about them. It didn't feel appropriate, though. They were still little more than acquaintances. She'd be mortified if they turned out to be vitamins.

A phone rang. Her phone. She was sure she'd switched it off before she'd put it in the safe, but there was no mistaking the ringtone. Odd. She pulled open the wardrobe door and knelt on the floor, tapped in the code and waited for the mechanism to hum. She reached in and saw she'd just missed a call from her housemate, Steve. Lily debated whether to call him back. They weren't supposed to use their phones. She'd be breaking the rules. Elliot had made that very clear, and the last thing Lily wanted was to be disqualified for cheating.

A message flashed up.

Sorry, forgot you were away. Nothing urgent. See you tomorrow x.

Problem solved, no emergency. Although now she had her phone and the display showed an available Internet connection. This would be the perfect opportunity to do some quick research on the other guests. No one would know, and she'd already decided who she was going to accuse. She chewed the inside of her lip. Maybe she wasn't so virtuous after all.

Debbie mentioned something earlier about the freedom of being switched off from the world. Lily hadn't understood at the time, but now she thought about it, she realised the phone was always with her and always on, even if she only got calls from family or Steve. When she was writing, she'd plug it in to charge on the far side of the room to stop herself from getting distracted. It didn't always work. Maybe she needed to get a safe.

No, she decided. She'd gain nothing by browsing the Internet now. She had confidence in her observations, and besides, once she opened her browser, she was bound to end up down a social media rabbit hole. She held the button at the top of the phone to make sure it was definitely off this time and settled it back on the soft fabric lining the safe. Lily pushed the sturdy metal door closed. As she stood, her tights snagged on the edge of the wardrobe, a long ladder creeping up her leg.

'Blast,' she said, and rummaged for the multi-pack she'd brought with her.

She tossed the ruined ones in the wastepaper bin in the corner and rolled the new and last pair up her legs. She slipped her feet into the Mary Janes and allowed herself another peek at her reflection. Lily wished she could look like this all the time, or at least a little less plain. Nothing she could do about that now. With a final swish of tassels, she stepped back out into the hall, ready to reveal the killer.

Lily made her way across the empty landing and towards the sweeping stairs, past the portrait of the man with an uncanny resemblance to Elliot and the vase of carnations underneath. She placed her hand on the smooth wooden banister and was about to descend when she paused. With the other guests still in their rooms, it was tranquil, but not silent. Clocks ticked, the house creaked, steady rain battered the windows. Lily listened. There was another sound too, a muffled sound inside the wall. She reminded herself that while eavesdropping wasn't in her nature, she could justify her actions a second time as being part of the game. She cupped her hand against the wall next to a tapestry and inclined her head to listen. They must be in one of the hidden servant passages. The voices were familiar.

'Who'd you wanna put your money on?' It was Elliot, and she'd been right about his fake accent. Even without it, there was no mistaking him. 'I vote Lily.'

She hoped that meant he thought she'd be the winner and not the one accused of being the murderer. It shouldn't matter, but it did.

She should step away. She glanced up, checking the corridor. No one else was coming out of their rooms, so instead she shuffled even closer to the wall and cupped her other hand against the wallpaper.

Jamie teased. 'You like her.'

Lily's cheeks flushed. She liked Elliot too. She'd never met anyone as charming, kind and quiet without being at all dull. He was a gentleman, with or without his silly accent. And like a gentleman, he deflected Jamie's question back to him.

'I'm spending all this time with them. I like all the guests. Anyway, who do you think it is?'

Jamie's response was more guarded. 'Too close to call. You'd better meet them for drinks. I'll pop down to the kitchen and check dinner's on time.'

A jostling inside the wall made her pull back. She wasn't quick enough, and Elliot appeared from a hidden door in the panelling to the side of a large tapestry. He almost walked straight into her. She pivoted and pretended to enjoy the scent of the flowers as much as she'd actually enjoyed them earlier. She couldn't tell who was more disconcerted, her for being caught listening or him for being caught out of character.

Elliot stuttered. 'Oh. Sorry.' He straightened his tie. 'Did you hear? Oh. You weren't supposed to hear any of that.'

He'd forgotten to go back into character and spoke with a slight Estuary twang. She liked his normal voice. Much more authentic to his personality.

Lily brushed her hair away from her face as she forced herself to focus on him, captivated by his dark eyes, but not sure what to say. She didn't need to make him feel bad for slipping out of character. It wouldn't ruin the game, and so she did something she never would have thought herself capable of.

She slipped her arm through his, gave herself a temporary aristocratic accent, and said, 'How fortuitous that we happened to meet. I was hoping for accompaniment to a grand cocktail reception.'

He stood tall, moved his shoulders back, his head held high, and became lord of the manor once more. 'Yes, one would be delighted to oblige.'

They made their way down the wide staircase, him with his arm crooked in front of him, her holding on to it. The butler held a silver tray of drinks. Elliot reached for a tall glass of sparkling water and gave it to Lily.

'Thank you.'

She melted into the background as Elliot greeted the other guests who'd come behind them. Lily watched him for just longer than necessary before she took a seat. She crossed her feet at her ankles and tucked them under the chair, wondering what else would appear different after the weekend finished.

Max unbuttoned his suit jacket and joined her. 'Penny for them.'

She gave him a nudge with her shoulder. 'No one says that anymore.'

He didn't bite. 'All set?'

'I think so. It's gone so quickly. I'm excited to see who's going to win.'

Only a few hours remained before there'd be a murderer and a winner. The game would be over and real life would resume. Lily wasn't sure she was ready for either.

CHAPTER 23

An angry roll of thunder accompanied Debbie as she entered the drawing room. She requested a Martini from the butler and sought Carol and Harvey, who'd huddled together in a corner.

Carol sipped her champagne. 'Are we all decided?'

Debbie confirmed. 'I think we are.'

'Me too,' Harvey said with unabashed delight.

Elliot circled the room. He exchanged pleasantries with Arthur and Grace seated on the sofa, then with Max and Lily against the far wall. Even he appeared to hesitate before he approached the ever-solitary Kevin, who once again gripped his cherished red wine. A dismal sight.

The grandfather clock in the hall chimed, which excused Elliot from making small talk with Kevin. Instead, he made his way back to his post, behind the large desk, where they'd all signed the guest book the day before. Debbie recognised his demeanour, one of a man about to give a presentation and not entirely comfortable about it. He knocked on the polished surface of the desk, then held his fist in front of his mouth and coughed a small, polite cough.

Debbie decided to help him out. He'd never get anyone's attention like that. 'If I can have a moment, everyone.' She gave two sharp claps. 'I believe Elliot has something to say.'

The obedience was immediate. The others followed her instruction, stopped their conversations to listen to whatever Elliot was about to say.

He shifted his weight from one foot to the other. 'Thank you, Debbie.'

She considered whether she'd made a mistake. Maybe the soft cough had been part of the performance. Too late now, and Elliot carried on unperturbed. He pulled open a drawer and removed a stack of white envelopes, before lining a row of pencils along the side of the table. He lifted open the top envelope and presented the card inside to the room. Debbie was close enough to see each of their names printed in capital letters next to a box.

'Oh, they're for voting,' Carol said.

'Correct,' Elliot said. 'If you'd like to put a cross next to the name of the guest you believe is the murderer, then seal it and slip it into this box.' He bent to retrieve a black, ballot-style container from beneath the desk. 'Then we'll go through to dinner, and we'll announce who's won.'

'Jolly good.' Arthur crossed the room and collected envelopes for him and Grace. Debbie broke away from Carol and Harvey. The time for teamwork had passed. The guests' expressions were serious as they each committed their final accusation to paper. Max strode across the room to be the first to cast his vote, closely followed by Lily.

Grace sealed her envelope and handed it to Arthur. He deposited them both and patted the top of the box. Debbie gave the old timer a wink as they crossed paths. Arthur ignored her.

The butler replenished his silver tray of drinks and circled the guests. Kevin, true to form, didn't wait to be asked and took one, drinking it down in two gulps. It appeared he intended to repeat his drunken behaviour from the night before, and Debbie suspected she'd be stuck sitting next to him again.

With the voting ritual complete, Elliot swung open the double doors to the dining room with the perfect amount of dramatic flair, and the guests filed in behind him. As she'd feared, the seating arrangement remained the same as the previous night, with only one exception. Jamie's setting was absent. Debbie was to be lumbered with Kevin again. She groaned.

A black sleeved arm reached around her and presented a shallow bowl of soup.

She breathed in spicy vegetable steam and selected a piece of warm artisan bread from the basket. She broke off a corner and watched the butter melt as she added it. She pushed her spoon through the soup and sipped, savouring it. Once again, the food was superb. She couldn't fault it.

'So,' Elliot said. 'The time has come to share what conclusions you've all come to.' Debbie nibbled her roll, choosing not to be first.

Arthur had no such reticence. 'We spotted the significance of the number eight fairly early on.'

His face lit up with pure delight. Such an obvious theme, conspicuous in the furniture, artwork and even some words and phrases Elliot used. She'd be amazed if the others hadn't worked that out too. She certainly had.

Kevin took a slug of wine. Fortified, he was off again. 'The body was arranged like someone used the hammer to strike it from behind, but Jamie's fingertips were stained a deep burgundy. So, I think they used the hammer to make it look like blunt force trauma, but poison is more likely.'

Curious. Debbie tried to keep the surprise out of her voice. 'How on earth do you know that?'

Arthur, ever the police expert, jumped in to corroborate his statement. 'He's correct. Fingertip staining was commonly used to identify victims of poisoning. Originated in the eighth century, I believe.'

Kevin glowed with wine or with pride. Debbie couldn't tell. Didn't care.

'I found a book open on the table in the library that explained it all,' he said. 'It was quite interesting, actually.'

The butler cleared the soup and served more wine.

Kevin's flushed face turned a mottled claret colour, not dissimilar to the wine he favoured. Debbie had struggled to keep her patience with him earlier that day, and expected she wouldn't be the only one to accuse him later. She genuinely hoped his disagreeable nature was a character trait he put on for the sake of the mystery. Even at the dinner table, he'd excluded himself, choosing to lean back in his chair now he'd made his little contribution, and instead of participating properly, he simply added the odd snide comment here and there. She supposed that in any group, there tended to be an outlier. One who distanced themselves for a particular reason, often lack of confidence or common interest, and if he'd just sat there quietly, that would have been fine. Instead, the bite-sized criticisms wore down her patience.

She snapped and spoke to him with unrestrained frustration. 'Seriously. If it's all so disagreeable to you, why did you even come?'

She realised she was speaking to him like she was telling him off. She rarely talked to anyone like that. Unless she wanted them to resign. An uncomfortable silence settled around the table. The others listened, watched, but didn't get involved.

Kevin fiddled with the serviette on his lap. His eyes darted from side to side, looking for an escape. 'Sorry. Honestly, I just came on this weekend to get some time away from the wife. I hadn't expected the murder would be so authentic, and it's worrying me. What if it was real and we're all running around like fools while Jamie's body's hidden in the walls somewhere and the murderer is about to come after us all?'

'I can assure you, that's not the case,' Elliot said.

Debbie tried to control her laughter. It took some effort. 'No, I'm sorry,' she said. 'That's the funniest thing I've heard all weekend. I'm sure we're perfectly safe.'

Carol giggled and patted her hair. Kevin's skin transitioned from claret to purple.

Debbie swished her hand in front of her face as she tried to contain herself. Tears of laughter threatened to spill. 'Honestly. Take no notice. It's a good thing you're so immersed in the weekend and we shouldn't laugh.'

Kevin scowled, unappeased. The oblivious butler brought out the main course. Kevin pushed it away with the heel of his hand: chargrilled steak accompanied by thick-cut chips. From what he'd said, he'd never indulge in such luxurious food at home.

His fear overcame him. 'It's in the food. The poison. You're all against me. Don't think I don't know. I'm not falling for it and I won't be the next to die.'

As he shoved the plate away, he knocked a jug of peppercorn sauce over the table. He waved at the butler in that rude manner he favoured when he wanted more wine. Drunk already. His wife's life must be miserable. No wonder she'd gone away without him this weekend. Probably needed a break.

Debbie forced herself to take a deep breath, collect herself, and stop laughing. She rubbed beneath her eye to check her mascara hadn't run, then picked up a chip and bit into it. Crisp on the outside, with a hot and fluffy centre. Pitiful. Kevin wasn't just irritating, he was paranoid, and his steak was going to waste.

On his other side, Lily concentrated on her meal. She sliced her steak into small pieces and chewed carefully. She did that most British of things when an uncomfortable situation presented itself and pretended she wasn't sitting right next to it. Debbie chuckled to herself as she tried to imagine what Lily would be like if she ever got angry. Lily peeked up from her plate and gave her a small smile, like she could read her thoughts.

'I think that's quite enough for now.' Carol reprimanded Debbie and Kevin like they were naughty children. 'Let's be civil and review what we've uncovered. Arthur, Grace, would you like to go first?'

Arthur didn't need to be asked twice. 'Hmm, we all spotted the theme of eight, I'm sure.' He pulled out the battered police notebook he'd been jotting in all day. 'We've followed that clue to a slightly different conclusion, and I'm sorry to say we believe Harvey is the culprit.'

Arthur stretched forwards to give Harvey an apologetic grimace. Harvey, for once, seemed lost for words.

Arthur picked up momentum. If nothing else, he was a determined old man. 'Yes, well, you let slip you wore the number eight shirt in the school rugby team and none of the other guests have any direct connection to the number, so it was a simple deduction.'

'Did I?' Harvey frowned. 'I don't remember that.'

'You mentioned it earlier. Don't worry, dear,' Grace said. 'We're none of us as fit as we used to be.'

Arthur found his flow. As he covered each point in his notebook, he licked the end of the small pencil and made a tick next to the note. He reached the end of his proclamation and paused for dramatic effect. 'And considering the route you would have taken to get here, I can only deduce you travelled on the number eight bus.' He had almost risen to a standing position as he spoke, and now recovered himself and lowered back down, scanning the others' faces for their reactions.

'Bravo!' Elliot exclaimed. Neither confirming nor denying their conclusion. Harvey wriggled in his chair, his brow damp as he searched for a place to deflect the suspicion.

He made his decision and raised a shaky hand, pointing towards Lily. 'I accuse Lily. She's the least likely to be the killer, and we all know it's always the one you least suspect.' He kept going, without punctuation. 'She's kind and quiet and watchful and nice.'

Lily studied the half-eaten steak in front of her, then chuckled. 'There's a compliment in there somewhere. I'll take it.'

Still, Debbie held back. This was not the time to show her hand. She wanted the others to go first, then she would swoop in and win. The weekend had proved to be fun, after all. She watched Max expectantly, fully intending he would take the hint and go next, but before they could continue, the butler interrupted by clearing away the main course. He piled the crockery up and carried it away. He served more wine.

Debbie kept her eyes firmly on Max.

CHAPTER 24

D ebbie stared at him in that way rich people do when they want you to do something. Max wasn't having any of it, and refused to give her the satisfaction of meeting her eye. In the background, the grandfather clock chimed eight. He was sure it'd already chimed eight once that evening. Nobody else seemed to notice, so he decided not to mention it. Most of the others were still busy throwing blame at each other. All a bit melodramatic for his liking and not something he'd get involved in until absolutely necessary.

He'd experienced a full range of emotions this weekend, for sure. From fear to enjoyment, and now overwhelm. Regardless of Debbie's prompting, he'd give his deductions any minute. No problem. Turned out, Theo had been right one last time. It was good for him to spend time with people, even if this setting was a surreal choice.

Lily spooned the last of her dessert into her mouth, a creamy, crunchy, Eaton mess that was a bit on the sweet side for his taste, but that she'd devoured.

Debbie had declined the dessert. 'Soy allergy,' she said. 'I avoid ice cream, just to be on the safe side.'

Max chuckled as Lily gazed longingly at the rejected meringue. She settled her spoon in the empty bowl. 'That was delicious.'

She dabbed her serviette at the corners of her mouth and tried to show Carol she needed to do the same.

The high drama of the allegations settled and now people were randomly shouting out all the references to the number eight they'd found. Carol was particularly pleased to have noticed the octagonal mirror by the front door. No one else got that. She acted like the clues were more important than the reveal itself.

The butler removed Max's half-finished dessert and settled a coffee cup and saucer in front of him. It was way too late to drink caffeine if he was going to stand any chance of sleeping tonight, so he nudged the cup to one side and picked up the square of mint chocolate from the saucer, popping it into his mouth, whole.

Having delivered the coffee, the solemn butler returned with the voting box and put it next to Elliot. He took half a step back. Max didn't get the purpose of the box, when they were all yelling out their findings anyway. This wasn't the calm, sophisticated finale you expected in a novel or a film, but even he had to admit it was pretty entertaining. Debbie had accused Kevin, and Carol shouted her agreement with disproportionate venom. Kevin roused himself enough to slur his own charge towards Harvey. Eventually, Max couldn't avoid making his case any longer and accused Arthur, explaining that, as an ex-police officer, he was the most likely to know how to commit a crime and get away with it. Only Lily stayed silent.

Elliot prompted her. 'Lily. Your turn please.'

Her hands shook as she contemplated what she was about to say. She whispered, 'Kevin. I think it's Kevin.'

Elliot opened the flap on the box and removed the white envelopes. He stacked them in front of him and checked his pocket watch.

Kevin, oblivious to the number of votes he'd accumulated, swayed in his chair. Max would have to say something soon, get the guy to bed and let him sleep it off. Maybe they could speak in the morning and Max could see about getting him some help. Fair play if it was all an act for the weekend, but he didn't think it was. The butler left the wine bottle on the table next to him. Kevin might as well be drinking straight from it.

The man had come up in discussion a lot over the past few days. Max tried to be sympathetic. There was a tinge of melancholy about him, something in that anger that Max couldn't put his finger on. He'd mentioned a wife, but no children. Maybe that was it, and he'd said she'd gone away without him. Maybe she'd left him, and he'd only find out when he got home. That was a cruel thought. Max reminded himself no one deserved to be alone. He knew how difficult that was, too.

Kevin's swaying intensified. He rocked to one side, still holding his wine. Just as he was about to fall, he stabilised himself and took another gulp, gripping the table with his free hand. He rocked to the other side. Coughed a loud, choking cough. Spluttering. They all stopped talking. Kevin fell. Max tried to catch him. Not quick enough, and Kevin slipped from consciousness onto the floor, still holding on to the tablecloth. Red wine sloshed over the table, the floor, and his trousers. His coffee cup and saucer crashed; his mint chocolate landed next to his hand as if waiting to be picked up and eaten. He lay crumpled on his side, the chair upturned, surrounded by debris from the table.

Carol screamed. Arthur stood to attention. Neither moved from their places at the table. Neither offered to help. Next to Max, Lily wedged her hands under her thighs. Someone needed to take control. He steeled himself, knowing he'd step up if need be. It wasn't like this was the first time he'd dealt with someone who'd had a bit too much to drink; sadly, the affliction often started a lot younger than people realised. He held back, still not entirely sure if this was part of the game.

Theo used to say that in moments of crisis, a person's true character surfaces. This was one of those times. Max prepared himself to step in, but it wasn't him to take charge of the situation, or even Debbie. Harvey's instinct had taken over. Instead of screaming or freezing or over-thinking, he moved without a word and knelt by Kevin's side. He angled his face so his cheek hovered over the other man's mouth and nose, checked for breathing, watched his chest to see if it moved. He rested two fingers with slight pressure on Kevin's neck, feeling for a pulse, and waited. The room held its breath.

Harvey sat back on his heels. 'Can someone call an ambulance, please?'

Lily pulled herself together and pushed back in her chair.

Elliot dropped to the floor, his flustered appearance contrasting with Harvey's calm demeanour. 'This isn't in the script,' he said.

Max eased Elliot out of the way and knelt with Harvey. The two of them worked together, trying to resuscitate Kevin. Max called out the count as he administered compressions.

Behind him, Lily also acted. 'I'll get my phone.'

She dashed out to the hall and collided with Jamie.

CHAPTER 25

J amie grasped Lily's shoulders. 'What's going on?'

'Kevin's unconscious.' She wriggled in his grasp.

'Well.' He spun her around. 'Let's go and see what's been happening and I'll sort it out.' Jamie gave her the slightest shove forwards, glad she complied. He knew exactly what was happening. He'd been watching, and as Kevin dropped to the floor, he'd already been halfway down the servants' stairs. No need for him to be hidden away any longer. Time he took back control.

As he followed Lily into the dining room, he spotted Debbie folding her arms and he asked his question again, this time to her. 'What's happened here?'

'More to the point,' Debbie said. 'Where have you been hiding?'

Jamie hated it when people answered a question with a question.

'Secret passages,' he said.

He moved round the table, stepping over the broken glass, and peered over Elliot at Kevin's form.

'But you're dead.' Carol picked at the remaining polish from her nails, flecks of red falling to the floor.

'Seriously?' Jamie struggled to keep the sarcasm out of his voice. 'Stop with the hysterics. It's not endearing.'

Carol pulled her chin back into herself and lowered back down with a thud.

Elliot gave him a warning stare, but Jamie wasn't in the mood to heed his orders anymore. Carol patted her hair.

Arthur flipped open his notebook as if it were all still part of the game. 'Look, we all know you've been hiding since your performance. I think it's time you shared a bit about where you've been and what you've been doing all day. Between us, we've carried out a thorough investigation of each other, but none of us knows anything about you.'

Jamie put his hands in his pockets. 'Personally, I'd suggest we have more pressing matters to deal with.' He fluttered his hand towards Kevin and the resuscitation efforts that were still underway, but had slowed. 'Considering the circumstances, the game is postponed. I've called the emergency services. They'll be here soon, and I'm sure Kevin will be fine once he's slept it off.'

Jamie knew Elliot had more gravitas with the guests than he did, he'd not spent as much time with them as his partner had, but he couldn't help being annoyed that instead of listening to him, they were all gawping at Elliot, waiting for confirmation.

Harvey and Max swapped places, counting, breathing, compressing. Jamie opted to supervise rather than interrupt their rhythm. He stood at the head of the table and gripped the back of the chair. In the same tweed suit as he'd worn the day before, just yesterday, when they'd all arrived, full of expectation about the weekend. Except he'd forgotten to change out of the trainers and back into the Oxfords. Damn. It didn't matter now. They'd spot them or they wouldn't, like pretty much everything else this weekend.

He folded his arms across his chest and addressed the room. 'I appreciate this is a shock. If one of you set out to hurt this man, now is the time to confess. The police will go easier on you all if you're a bit more honest about the whole thing.' He turned to Lily for no particular reason other than she was in his line of sight, still hovering by the double doors. 'Was it you?'

Lily whimpered. 'What are you talking about?' she said. 'Kevin's just had too much to drink. This is all getting muddled. I'm sure once the ambulance gets here, they can sort him out.'

Thunder rolled outside. The lights flickered.

'Assuming they can get here in the storm.' Debbie twisted her ring as she stated the obvious.

Jamie bit back his reply. He wanted to push them all to find out how far they'd go, but he didn't. He waited. Sometimes silence was the most powerful tool you had. Debbie had taught him that.

The brave and broken Max picked up the challenge between compressions. 'You need to stop throwing accusations around and do some explaining. This isn't what the paying public will expect, and I doubt the police will let you continue to operate if there's been an actual death on the premises.'

His eyes narrowed and Jamie half expected him to come over and confront him, to use his size to intimidate. Instead, he took a long slow breath, keeping his composure, and waited for a response.

'You're right,' Jamie said. 'First, we need to get this man some help, and then we all need to sit down and fess up.'

Elliot, still on the floor, crestfallen. Poor, trusting Elliot, who'd always been with him, always supported him.

Arthur interjected. 'Max makes a valid point. It's time you both explained what's going on. This weekend's a sham. The clues were far too simple and now we're on the cusp of having a genuine death to deal with. We've no phones and only your word that the emergency services are on their way. Add to that, the distinct possibility this will not stop with Kevin. We're all in danger.'

'That's ridiculous,' Debbie said. 'First off, we can get our phones whenever we like. Lily was about to do just that when you got in the way. We can also leave whenever we want to. I'm sure the ambulance coordinators would have warned us if their attendance was going to be hindered by the rain, so I shouldn't think the storm is anywhere near as bad as it sounds.' She crossed her legs and swung her foot up and down. 'And third, Kevin has just had too much to drink. There's no reason whatsoever to think anyone else with a bit more self-control will be in any danger at all.'

'Really?' Arthur pointed at the mantelpiece. 'Then how would you explain the swans?'

CHAPTER 26

Lily followed Arthur's gaze, and there they were. Seven candles carved in the shape of swans were 'swimming' along the mantelpiece.

'I'm positive those weren't there before,' he said, and she agreed. There was no way, during all their investigations that weekend, that the entire group would have missed them. There was no way she would have missed them.

Lily rubbed the goosebumps on her exposed arms. The emerald dress she loved so much now revealed itself as impractical. She craved her jeans, her sensible shoes and her magnolia room. She should've gone to the pub with Steve.

Harvey's resuscitation efforts slowed. 'I think we've lost him.' He sounded dejected.

Max carried on, his face set in determination. 'We can't stop until the paramedics get here,' he said. 'We can swap places again if you need to.'

Elliot put his hand on Harvey's shoulder in a gesture that both acknowledged his efforts and gave him permission to rest. He took Harvey's place himself and settled into the rhythm with Max.

Harvey used the back of a chair to pull himself up. He wheezed. His shirt was untucked at the front and peppercorn sauce stained the knee of his trousers. He swapped persona from first aider to mystery sleuth and addressed Arthur.

'The setup's right.' He rubbed the side of his face as he equated swans with the imminent danger they represented. 'There's no obvious connection between us as guests, and no single motive I've spotted.' He scanned the room, inviting someone to disagree. 'That is, unless we're looking for a hidden secret, which, let's be honest, we all have.'

'Doesn't everyone?' Arthur tapped his pencil against his bottom lip, speaking to himself. 'The only thing we know we have in common is an interest in mystery. That's tenuous as a motive for murder. Let's just hope the emergency services arrive soon. I'm sure they'll sort it all out.'

'Honestly,' Debbie said. 'Swans or no swans, there's no reason to suspect foul play and I, for one, am disappointed. I'm sure I speak for the rest of us when I say I was rather bought into the whole thing and would like to find out who did it. Once Kevin's got professional help, the rest of us can carry on.'

Debbie's giant diamond sparkled in the candlelight.

Carol shifted in her chair and Debbie paused to let her speak. 'How long do you think they'll be, anyway?'

'Not long,' Elliot said, then addressed Jamie. 'Can you take over for a minute, please?'

Jamie knelt without a word and Elliot slipped out to the drawing room.

Lily whispered to Grace. 'Should we follow him?'

'No, dear, let him be.'

She was right, but Lily couldn't bear to just wait there next to the body. How quickly a man with a name and a life became just 'the body'. How quickly things changed. She moved round to the other side of the table where she couldn't see Max and Jamie as they kept working on reviving Kevin. It didn't help. She could still hear them, counting, compressing.

Elliot knocked his elbow on the door frame as he hurried back in. He'd been behind the scenes somewhere and brought a mobile phone back with him. Elliot Windsor, host and gentleman of the manor, was still there somehow, doing his best to stay calm and to make it all okay.

'I've just tried to call the ambulance and see what's taking them so long,' he said. 'The storm's still pretty fierce and it's knocked out the phone signal.'

'It's fine.' Jamie sounded miffed. 'I already called them from the phone in the office. I'm sure they won't be much longer.'

Debbie cupped her elbow with one hand and drummed her fingers on the table.

Arthur scratched his musings into his notebook, pausing now and then to show them to Grace. After he'd repeated the process a few times, he straightened. 'If we're certain we can't do anything else for Kevin, and anyone harbours the slightest suspicion something untoward has taken place, I think we should leave the scene. We're risking contamination the longer we're here, and besides, we'll be in the way when the professionals arrive.'

Carol gripped the table. 'We can't leave him.' She challenged the others, looking horrified. 'I know none of us gelled with Kevin, but that doesn't mean I don't want to stay with him until help arrives.'

They fidgeted. None of them knew what to do. Whether they should stand, or sit, stay in this room, or move to the next. The dining room, once so warm and inviting, now felt stuffy. Lily's throat was dry. She reached across to get her drink and used both hands to steady it. Her mind raced. So much for a fun puzzle. Now someone had been hurt, and although she was fairly confident this wasn't part of the game; like Debbie, she couldn't help but be disappointed and, in turn, that made her feel guilty. The ambulance would be there soon. She knew it would. It had to be. She drank more water. Her hands were a little more steady at least; small mercy. The grandfather clock chimed seven.

CHAPTER 27

Debbie got up from the table and paced, moving back and forth along the wall furthest from Kevin. She always paced when she needed to think. Something about the steady movement helped her concentrate, and at this particular moment in time, that's exactly what she needed to do. She folded her arms across her chest, lowered her head in contemplation, focused, and paced.

No one seemed to be in charge. Debbie normally preferred to adopt the role herself. She'd learned over the years that when you have a desired outcome in mind, it's often better to take the lead. Still, as long as someone directed proceedings, she could cope. What she disliked more than anything were situations where no one was in control. Like now.

The so-called hosts should be stepping up, not watching from the sidelines. A couple of calls to the emergency services and a lacklustre attempt at CPR wasn't her definition of taking command, and that incompetent butler was little more than a glorified drinks machine. Could be an actor, that would explain it. As soon as the paramedics arrived to take the body away, she'd give this whole thing up as a bad loss and go home. Such a disappointment. She'd bought into the idea of holding her team event here and had allowed herself to enjoy the prospect of swaying through the egos of her colleagues as they competed for her esteem. Such a pity. She should have known it was too good to be true. A perfect event, just falling into her lap the way it did. Now the ever-diligent Milly would need to spend yet more hours pulling research papers together and she would need to review them and choose an alternative. How utterly tiresome.

Her laptop remained dutifully locked away upstairs. Not ideal. This seemed like the perfect opportunity to catch up on the work she'd missed this weekend. Surely there could be no objections if she nipped out to get it. Just until the police arrived. She'd be able to crack on with her presentation for next week, provide the police with her statement, and still be home before midnight. Assuming the storm didn't hold them up. It was only a bit of rain after all, even if it had knocked out the mobile phone reception.

A bell chimed. Debbie stopped mid-step. The room smelled of adrenaline. It reminded her of the board room when prospective suppliers trailed in, hoping to impress. The guests' attention focused on the exit, and the butler, who'd been loitering in the corner by the clock like some sort of lost ornament, went to admit the cavalry.

Two paramedics hastened through the door, one male, one female, dressed in green trousers and short-sleeved shirts. They ignored their audience and dropped to the side of the patient. Jamie and Max moved aside. Flat metal scissors cut open Kevin's shirt to reveal grey wisps of chest hair. They checked his airway, they checked his pulse, they stuck pads onto his torso and shouted for the room to 'stand clear'. The machine whirred and compelled its charge into Kevin, pulling up his chest. After the shock came more checking, then another shock, and another. They were all hypnotised by the efforts of the medical staff.

After an indeterminate amount of time, the male paramedic confirmed the news. 'It's too late, I'm afraid,' he said to no one in particular. 'We've done everything we can. We're sorry for your loss.'

They packed the equipment into a large green bag. The guests watched, hypnotised by the drama. When a solitary policeman strolled in, Carol, who'd become increasingly skittish, let out yet another gasp. Her constant giggling and gasping grated on Debbie, but at least someone with a semblance of authority had finally arrived.

The compact police officer was shorter than she expected, although she wasn't sure why, and he did have a tinge of natural authority that she appreciated. He wore a dark navy uniform, almost black, the tunic adorned with silver buttons, each embossed with a crown. He carried his helmet in the crook of his arm. The bottom of his trousers and his shoes were soaked.

The room collectively waited for instruction, and the officer obliged. His tone was authoritative, yet polite, and gave no suggestion of choice. 'Ladies and gentlemen, until we confirm otherwise, we'll be treating this room as a crime scene.' He rocked on his heels and gestured to the double doors. 'If you could all move through to the drawing room, we'll let the medical professionals finish their work.'

'How awful,' Carol said as she filed behind Max.

Debbie spotted Arthur's smug expression, pleased with himself for calling out the potential need for further investigation. He checked himself and complied with the instructions of the officer without a word. Grace slipped her arm through his and passed through the double doors. Debbie went last, pleased to leave, although she wouldn't be admitting that to the others. She might be strong, but even she preferred not to be trapped in a room with a dead body.

No one looked back.

The drawing room had been the epicentre of the entire weekend. It's where they'd all come in, signed the guest book and later committed their allegations to paper.

Arthur and Grace claimed the large sofa. Lily, the chair next to them; and Harvey and Carol sank into the armchairs on either side of the fireplace like some sort of mismatched bookends.

More intolerable waiting. She could be working instead of hanging around at this failed event. She twisted her ring, determined once more to keep her patience.

Elliot slunk behind the desk. His fingertips rested on the leather writing block as if that were the only thing holding him up. His features were drawn, his skin had an odd grey tinge.

The policeman stood in front of the fireplace and reached into his front pocket. He pulled out a long dark notepad, not dissimilar to the one Arthur carried around with him. He pulled a small wooden pencil from the loop on the side and passed from one guest to the next, neither inviting nor discouraging them to speak. Someone was always the first to talk if you let the silence hang long enough, and Arthur took that as his cue. Judging that, as the fellow crime professional in the room, he had a duty to speak up. How ironic. He had the audacity to explain the setup of the murder mystery weekend as though it were his own construct. As if it were relevant.

He cleared his throat. 'None of us know each other,' he said. 'Except for myself and Grace, of course.' He gazed down at her with a mixture of love and reverence.

Of course, the perfect couple, gallantry and glamour, a lifetime of love and experience, too long, too upstanding, to be involved in anything unsavoury. A lifetime of do-gooding and duty.

The officer scratched a few notes. 'Thank you, sir. That's very useful.'

The old man beamed. The officer moved on to Max, who squared his shoulders and kept all but a touch of defiance from his voice.

'I didn't know him either.'

The officer raised an eyebrow, expectant. 'Let me re-phrase. Explain for me what interactions you had with the deceased.'

The silence hung in the air. Max stood his ground. Good for him. Debbie could tell he wanted to back away.

'None that I can think of,' Max said. 'Most of us have been getting to know each other, enjoying working out the clues for the game. Kevin kept himself to himself, like he didn't want to be here.'

The officer persisted. 'And how did *you* come to be here?'

'I was invited.' Max's jaw clenched.

'We all were,' Lily said.

The officer asked them all variations of the same questions. When he was done, he flipped the notepad shut and slipped the pencil into the holder at the side. 'I'd like to request you all remain on the premises for the time being. The forensic team will be here shortly and will want to take samples for elimination purposes. We'll tape off the room, but otherwise you can carry on as normal. I'll arrange transportation in the morning.'

'Nothing about this is normal,' Carol said, missing the point as usual.

'Explain to me why we need to wait until tomorrow.' Debbie clenched her fist until her nails dug into her palm.

'Most of our resources are busy dealing with the effects of this storm.' The officer tucked his notepad into his inside pocket. 'It's forecast to get worse before it gets better, but when it's passed over, I'd like you all to come to the station to make formal statements. Try to get some rest in the meantime.'

'Thank you, Officer.' Elliot shook his hand and showed him out. He'd forgotten his helmet, still on the side. Debbie ignored it. She was in no mood to be helpful.

Jamie took a step forwards. 'If we're stuck here for a while, I think a brandy is in order.' Debbie couldn't agree more.

CHAPTER 28

Lily warmed her hands by the fire as Jamie decanted brandy and passed it around to everyone except her, Max and the butler, who stayed in character despite the change in circumstances. There was no need to pretend he was there to serve them anymore. But it wasn't her place to say, and if it gave him comfort to stay in character, it didn't do any harm.

Two crime scene investigators dressed in white overalls with blue plastic shoe covers rustled past. The taller of the two, a man with his hood up and a surgical mask hiding his face, pushed a metal stand with a large light on top. The other, a woman with strawberry blonde hair and impossibly high cheekbones, carried a white storage case. She caught Lily staring at her as she walked past, but didn't speak. Lily pulled a cushion onto her lap and hugged it.

Brilliant white light seeped under the double doors and Lily imagined the elegant period dining room stripped of its mystique by the clinical glare.

'Now there's one wasting her talents.' Debbie raised her brandy glass.

'Hmm?' Lily said.

'Brains might be brilliant for science, but with those features, she'd have been better matched to a career in sales. I just dread to think what these lab rats get paid, and she could make an absolute fortune in marketing.'

Debbie's single focus on business had impressed Lily when they first met, but had become draining. Lily bit the inside of her cheek. Debbie had judged the woman's appearance and read it all wrong. Although Lily only glimpsed her as she'd passed, it wasn't her features that didn't fit, it was her age. She was young.

Lily totted up the years of study and training that it must take to qualify and train. A little too young, perhaps.

Like she'd sensed she was being talked about, the woman joined them in the drawing room, lowered the white case on the floor and lifted the lid. She used her teeth to pull off the plastic strip at the top of an individual bag containing a cotton bud, leaving flecks of berry lipstick behind. Not exactly sterile, but then it was the result, not the packet, that was important, Lily supposed. The woman wiped the bud inside Debbie's cheek, no doubt collecting traces of brandy as much as DNA. She repeated the process with each of them in silence. It tickled, but wasn't unpleasant. When she'd collected seven cotton buds in the case, she snapped the lid shut and joined her colleague, all without saying a word.

A trolley covered with a green sheet squeaked past. The shape of a man underneath. The male scientist kept his hood tied snuggly around his chin and a surgical mask covered most of his face. There was something familiar about him. She couldn't place it and disregarded the thought. The blonde wheeled the light box away, and just like that, Kevin was gone.

Lily felt strangely relieved as the front door slammed and she knew his body was out of the manor.

The young scientist returned and smoothed yellow tape along the diagonal of the double doors. She spoke in a cheery voice. 'Please don't use this room until the police confirm they've gathered up any evidence,' she said.

The instruction was for them all, but Jamie jumped up. 'It goes without saying.'

He offered his hand for her to shake, and she placed her plastic-gloved hand in his. He escorted her to the front door.

Arthur tutted. 'This can't be proper procedure. Surely we should leave now. Give statements at the station, or go home and wait to be contacted. It's not just the dining room they need to investigate.'

'I wouldn't know.' Carol patted her hair. 'I've never been wrapped up in a murder investigation before.'

Grace slipped her arm through Arthur's and she spoke with her normal blend of kindness and patience. 'And it's been a long time since we've investigated any crimes. Things have moved on. Times change.'

'I agree,' Debbie said. 'Our options are limited, and we have to trust they know what they're doing. Personally, I don't fancy trying to get a cab in this weather, even though I'd much rather get home. We should do as we're asked, get some sleep, and leave first thing in the morning when we've given our statements.'

Arthur pursed his lips. Grace gave him a look that left no doubt who was in charge of their relationship, and he conceded.

'More importantly,' Debbie said. 'I'd like to discuss what safety precautions we can put in place. Whether there are additional keys to our rooms floating about, for example, and I'll certainly be retrieving my phone, so would appreciate the Wi-Fi code.'

'That sounds reasonable.' Elliot looked across to check with Jamie, who nodded his permission. 'I'll get you all the spare keys to your rooms.'

Carol and Harvey exchanged a guilty look. Maybe they'd already been poking around in the other guests' rooms. Just peeking into Max's earlier had felt like cheating to her. Elliot pushed a panel next to the bookcase. It swung open just enough to let him slip out of the servants' exit hidden behind. Lily had worked out ages ago that this must be where the staircase from upstairs led, but it captivated Harvey.

'Secret passage, one of the grand traditions of a mystery house.' He peered around the entrance and up the staircase, but didn't follow. Something held him back. Fear, or some misplaced politeness, Lily couldn't be sure.

Elliot's footsteps thumped as he returned, and with a solemn face, he provided copies of the heavy brass keys he'd used to unlock their doors the evening before. 'These are the only spares.'

Arthur accepted their key. 'Well, if we must stay the night, I intend to get an early start tomorrow, so we'll head up.' He and Grace moved together towards the wide hallway. The others followed. Max slipped his arm around Lily's shoulder and gave it a brief squeeze.

Jamie and Elliot stayed behind. She sympathised. They'd put so much into this weekend and whatever hope they'd fostered of scaling the business must be ruined now. Lily halted halfway up the stairs and looked back at their hosts. They'd collapsed into the armchairs by the fireplace, each lost in their own thoughts as they gazed at the flames. She realised neither of them had provided a DNA sample and wondered what it might mean. Maybe this was still part of the game after all.

CHAPTER 29

The fire dwindled. Jamie stretched his feet out in front of him and crossed them at the ankles. Elliot had failed to mention the reappearance of the trainers. That couldn't be a good sign.

'Well, that was a surprise,' he said.

Elliot stayed slumped in the chair, with the posture of a man who had nothing left to give; all pretence of being host evaporated. He screwed up his face like he was trying to process his thoughts, to work out how their business venture had gone so horribly wrong.

His voice cracked when he spoke. 'Please tell me you changed the plot without telling me and this is all part of some elaborate surprise I'll look back on in a few weeks and have a good laugh about.'

'Afraid not, old chap.' Poor Elliot, so used to life going his way. So lost when that wasn't the case. Kendrick Manor had taken over both of their lives. 'It will all work out. Like things always do.'

'Do you think it was an accident, or was Kevin murdered?'

'Hard to say,' Jamie said. 'How many of them guessed he was my killer?'

'About half.'

'Not bad.' Jamie stood and spun around on the spot. 'Anyway, we must stay focused.' He swept his arm theatrically in front of him. 'It was decreed that two men would construct a plot so elaborate, so cunning, that the participants would stumble through investigations, not knowing who the perpetrator was.'

Elliot's face was grey. 'Not now, Jamie. Not when everything we've worked for has all been destroyed. Someone's actually died. We could lose it all.'

Jamie propped an elbow on the mantelpiece. 'It's not like Kevin is so great a loss to the world.'

'That's not the point.'

'And what is the point? Do you think he was murdered? And who did that, and more importantly, how?'

'Honestly, I've no idea.' Elliot put his head in his hands. 'This wasn't in the script, and now I don't know what to think, or what to do. The police will shut us down. Our dream is over.'

He was right, in a way. This wasn't in the original script. When they'd planned the weekend, they'd decided one guest would play the part of the murderer. It was all top secret until they arrived and the individual would be allocated their role. All eight had an equal chance of being nominated, and as the rooms were allocated randomly, it was all down to luck. Jamie didn't believe in luck. When Elliot had greeted each guest and asked them to sign the book, he'd taken a key from the drawer of the desk and showed them to that room. So, when Kevin arrived, out of sorts from his experience with the minicab driver, chance decided he'd been given the Baker Street room. When he'd settled in, like all the other guests, to open his envelope, he'd read the same introductions they had, but he'd had an extra piece of paper handwritten in elaborate cursive. The words still rang true, and Jamie knew them off by heart.

Congratulations. We have selected you to play what is quite possibly the most important role of this weekend, that of the murderer. Your task is to avoid discovery by deflecting those clues and the suspicions of your fellow guests. Good luck.

Good luck indeed. Kevin had no luck at all, wretched man.

It was already the early hours of Sunday morning when the friends stepped behind the bookcase and climbed the servants' stairs to the attic. Jamie paused to speak to Elliot, but before he got the chance, Elliot closed his door. He went into the adjoining room. He could do with some rest as well. Jamie kicked off his trainers, exhausted. His father had always told him off when he did that after school, which somehow made him relish the action as an adult. He hung the tweed jacket with care on the coat hanger on the back of the door and laid the trousers across the top of the wooden chair in the corner. He could see his breath, but he didn't feel a chill. He lay on top of the covers on the single bed, stretched his arms above his head and stared at the ceiling, waiting for the sleep he knew wouldn't come. His whole body was alive with adrenaline as he processed the last few hours.

He imagined Elliot next door, changing into his traditional tartan pyjamas. The ones Jamie always thought made him look like an old man. He just needed a pair of corduroy slippers to complete the outfit. Jamie wondered if Elliot would struggle to sleep, too. Kevin had played the perfect murderer. They couldn't have chosen better if they'd tried. Such a shame things worked out how they did.

The manor fell asleep, waiting for the police to return and release them back into the world. Jamie lay in the dark, the steady beat of the rain outside accompanied by creaks from the old property, and slipped into semi-consciousness.

Tomorrow it would all be over.

CHAPTER 30

D ebbie changed into her pyjamas. The expensive peach satin brushed against her skin. She piled all the pillows behind her back in the shape of a V and pushed herself up in bed. Her fingers flew over the keys of the laptop she'd retrieved from the safe at the bottom of her wardrobe. Jamie had said the game was postponed, so she reasoned the no-technology rule must be too. Elliot wouldn't have given her the Wi-Fi code otherwise. Regardless, now there'd been an actual death, she had no intention of wasting any more time, or being without her beloved computer.

She should use the time to catch up on work. That presentation wouldn't finish itself, but her mind was too full of the events of the past few days and she needed to get all that thinking out of her head and written down properly. Log it, analyse it and understand what she was facing. Across the room, she'd left the brass key in the lock and she'd propped a chair against the handle like she'd seen on television. Whether it would stop an intruder, she had no idea, but it wouldn't make it any easier to get in and the physicality of it comforted her. She considered whether to drag the dresser across the door as well, but decided that was a little much.

She wasn't a nervous person as a rule, quite the opposite. Still, Kevin's untimely demise was sinister, to say the least, despite the slim possibility this was still part of the game. She twisted her ring. Being asked to stay overnight didn't make sense. Storm or no storm, it hadn't stopped the waiters leaving or the police getting there, so they weren't cut off. That was something, but the whole thing was increasingly inconvenient.

People tried to tell you that to be successful in business, you need qualifications, ruthlessness, or charm. Debbie, though, knew a lot of it was simply about perseverance and being organised. She'd always thrived on the uncertain, on change, and found it frustrating when those around her didn't pick up on things as quickly as she did. She applied the same level of logic to most aspects of her life and saw no reason the current circumstances shouldn't be treated in the same way. She also liked to win, and while the other guests were charming in their own little ways, they weren't cut out for problem-solving on this scale, and she was sceptical of the police at the best of times.

She still remembered their incompetence when a petty criminal had had the audacity to try to defraud her company. The emergency services. Now that was a joke. It took them forty-eight hours to send round a detective, if that's what you'd call him. He'd drunk cup after cup of builder's tea while he took individual statements from the staff, monopolising the boardroom for the best part of a day, only to leave them to wait a week for a report that the insurance company rejected anyway on the basis that the company had failed to follow proper measures. What an insult. They never found out who did it.

The laptop was light on her thighs, its warmth reassuring. On the screen, a spreadsheet where she'd listed all the guests on the front page, with links through to their individual summaries. She'd documented all the clues she could think of and allocated each a score. She'd included sheets for Jamie and Elliot. Her years in the corporate environment made her all too aware that those in charge of a company were often its biggest threat, and she had no intention of falling into the trap of excluding them from consideration. She'd also created sheets for each of the unnamed waiters. Eight of them too, she noted, and although they'd come and gone throughout the weekend, she didn't want to make the mistake of thinking they weren't important enough to be the culprits. She remembered the talk she'd given her team after her restructure. Reminding them how important each person was to the success of the company, regardless of how senior their role, telling them that 'no one is too important to make the tea'. She loved that saying. Obviously, she never made the tea, Milly did.

She reached over to the chilled brandy she'd brought up with her. Pretty decent bottle. She placed the heavy glass on the nightstand and contemplated the room. The printed wallpaper resembled a bank of typewriters and there was even a spiral staircase in the corner. It didn't lead anywhere. She'd checked. A catapult lay discarded on the dresser, next to a mask – neat little details that only a true mystery aficionado, like herself, would appreciate. Debbie felt at home in the office environment, possibly more at home than she did in her decadently designed house.

She considered which of the guests were connected with the various clues and wished she had her team with her to divvy up the work. Some of her analysts would make short shrift of compiling what she'd noted down and, while circumstances had changed somewhat since she'd arrived, she couldn't help but imagine the fictional part of the weekend being attended by those she worked with. She could visualise it, the perfect team activity. Such a shame. Even if Kevin's demise was from natural causes and not part of the plot, there was no way she could recommend the weekend now. It would never get past those health-and-safety tyrants.

She savoured the last of the brandy, leaving the remnants of an ice cube behind, and considered the clues she'd compiled. Nothing significant stood out. So frustrating. It could have been any of them. She checked the Internet again, hoping to connect. The blasted Wi-Fi was either down or non-existent, and the rain still interfered with her phone reception. Not the end of the world. She knew she'd find herself answering emails for the rest of the night if she could, and regardless of this mess, a few more hours without contact with work wouldn't kill her. Whatever was waiting for her, she'd deal with it in the morning. For now, she'd get some sleep and let her subconscious keep working on the problem. See what she came up with tomorrow. It was a tactic she'd often applied to work. She put the laptop and phone back in the safe, reorganised her pillows, and clicked off the bedside lamp.

She concentrated on slowing her breathing until she was no longer concentrating and fell into a dreamless sleep.

Until a scream jolted her upright.

CHAPTER 31

A scream. Lily yanked open her door and rushed towards the sound. She saw Debbie fling open her own door and the two women converged outside Grace and Arthur's room. Lily imagined herself through Debbie's eyes, how dishevelled she must look, her hair scraped back in a messy bun. She tugged at her cotton vest and tucked it into her lounge pants, taking in Debbie's designer silk, amazed that anyone wore nightwear like that in real life.

'You heard the scream?' Lily's breath was short. She could have kicked herself. Debbie wouldn't be there if she hadn't. She hated that she always felt so intimidated by this woman.

Debbie gave her a curt nod and rapped twice on the bedroom door. Her voice, as always, was a touch louder than it needed to be. 'Hello. Are you all right in there?' She knocked again, sharper this time. 'Hello. Grace. Arthur. It's Debbie. Lily's with me. We heard a scream and just want to make sure you're okay.'

A key rattled on the other side of the door, and the brass doorknob rotated. The weary woman who answered bore no resemblance to the glamorous Grace they'd become accustomed to. One arthritic hand gripped the door frame like she'd contracted frailty overnight. Her make-up-free face was now lined with age and distress, her face swollen and puffy, her skin red and blotchy.

'He's gone.'

Lily gathered Grace in her arms, and let her sob onto her chest. This time, there was no need for Debbie to give out instructions. Lily's instincts said her role was to care, and Debbie's was to investigate. She earned herself another nod, this one confirmation she'd acted as required. It didn't take a genius to work out the scream was something to do with Arthur, and Lily was comfortable letting Debbie lead the way on getting the details.

Lily steered Grace towards one of the upholstered chairs in the hallway. She crouched in front of her, gazing into the distraught face of the woman she'd become so fond of.

'Stay here,' she said. 'I'm going to help Debbie. If you need me, I'll just be a few seconds away.'

She searched Grace's face for confirmation and squeezed her hand. She didn't want to leave her, but there might be something they could do for Arthur, so she knew she must.

Debbie flicked a switch. Various lamps around the room came on all at the same time. The two women approached the bed with caution. Lily already suspected what they'd find. The covers were thrown back on one side, while the other remained neatly tucked around the form of a person. Arthur. Resting in peace. That was something. Apart from his open eyes, fixed on the ceiling. Lily didn't want to touch him, but somehow it felt disrespectful to leave him searching the ceiling for the answer to life's questions.

'Should we call an ambulance?' Lily said.

'We should. Although, I regret to say, I think Grace is right. I don't think he's with us anymore.'

She knelt beside the bed as if to pray and with respect lowered his lids for him in a gesture Lily found both moving and mortifying.

'Shouldn't we try to resuscitate him? I could get Max.' Lily could hear the urgency in her voice, even though she knew they were too late. Another death.

She stepped back from the bed and knocked a pile of papers on the desk covered in Arthur's neat handwriting. He'd listed the details he and Grace had gathered throughout the weekend. In between Arthur's printed words, another, more decorative, hand had written further notes. Lily picked up the top page where they'd noted their thoughts about Kevin. She suspected Grace had been the true brains in their relationship, and this proved it. Arthur focused on facts, the personal characteristics of the guests and the layout of the house, while Grace had added the seasoning, noting how each clue connected and what it might mean. Maybe this was how they'd always worked. Arthur, integral to the police force, with Grace behind him, showing him the way to the answers. It wouldn't be such a terrible thing if it were true. A partnership in every sense of the word. She wiped away a tear.

Debbie picked up the stack of notes, folded them, and slipped them into the large pocket on the front of her silk dressing gown. 'Let's move Grace somewhere else.' She patted Lily awkwardly on the back. 'We can read these and get Grace settled until the police arrive. I wouldn't mind giving them another ring and geeing them up.'

'I agree,' said Lily.

She didn't want to be in there any longer than necessary. Poor Arthur. The bedside table still held the book he'd been reading and would never finish, a glass of water and a bottle of pills. She'd seen a bottle like that somewhere before, but couldn't place it.

Debbie removed the key from the back of the door and pulled it closed, locking it and slipping the key into her pocket, along with the notes.

Grace hadn't moved from where they'd left her. She rocked in the chair, crying silent tears. Debbie was the one to say it, with genuine tenderness, making it real. 'I'm so sorry, Grace. He's passed. Let's take you downstairs and get you some tea.'

As they descended, the grandfather clock chimed six.

Back in the drawing room, yet again, Lily helped Grace to a chair by the fire. She took a tartan blanket from the back and tucked it across her lap, releasing the faint smell of smoke. The fire was nothing but embers. Someone had cleared the brandy glasses from the night before.

Lily squatted next to Grace and held her hand, cold and fragile. 'Do you want to talk about it? Tell us what happened?'

Grace gave her a sad half-smile, and, in a faltering voice, explained. 'We were so shocked about what happened to Kevin. I know he was a tad on the difficult side, but you wouldn't wish that on anyone. It's just all a bit off. The police officer asking us to stay, even the questions he asked.

'We all went up to bed at about the same time. I'd not even changed out of my eveningwear. My Arthur made me a cup of tea and wrapped a cardigan around my shoulders. It didn't match at all, but he always said I could wear anything and still be beautiful. He was such a charmer.' Grace sobbed.

Lily squeezed her hand. 'He was,' she said. Past tense.

'I watched Arthur make notes. It was just like the old days when he'd come home and we'd work through the problems together. He was such a marvellous man.' She hesitated, leaving a pause where someone might disagree and she would come to his defence. 'He'd ripped all the pages from that silly old police notebook and laid them in a neat line across the bedspread. He was still in his evening outfit too, except he'd taken off his tie and undone the top button of his shirt. He'd done the same at the end of every shift when he was still in the force. I always nagged him to get changed properly when he got home. He never did, argued there was no value in getting changed for a couple of hours, only to get changed again for bed.

'He ran through the list of all the information we'd gathered. Meticulous as always, and I refined; just a different perspective on the same information, you understand. He had most of it already, he always did.'

Lily caught Debbie's slow blink. They'd both noticed it was Grace who brought the real insight into their partnership. Lily couldn't help wondering what Arthur would have amounted to if it weren't for Grace. But then, he doted on her, so while he'd built a career on the back of her brilliance, he hadn't taken it, or her, for granted.

Grace continued. 'I'm embarrassed to say neither of us took to Kevin. He was such a disagreeable man and so bitter about so many things. It had to be more than just a character he was playing, we were sure. It seemed like he was broken and didn't know how to heal. We'd deduced the number eight pretty early on. I think we all picked up on that, and Harvey had the most connections. Then Kevin collapsed and was actually dead, so we realised there must be more to it. If it was a murder, and we still don't know it was, there would need to be a connection between Kevin and at least one of the other guests that went beyond the structure of the game. Someone would have to have known he was going to be here before the weekend started.'

Lily shivered and pulled a blanket around her own shoulders. Debbie either didn't feel or wouldn't acknowledge the cold. She rested her bare arm on the back of her chair.

Grace continued. 'We discounted ourselves, of course. A lifetime of complete honesty is a rare and valuable thing. We talked about you.' Her head tilted towards Debbie, whose eyes flared. 'You're so confident and purposeful, but we hardly know anything about you. Forgive me for saying, dear, but you don't give the impression you have much else in your life except your job.'

Debbie opened her mouth to speak, but Grace carried on and she closed it again. Good, this wasn't the time.

'Anyway, we dressed for bed. I hung our clothes in the wardrobe. We discussed what happened, reviewed the suspect list. Arthur gathered the notes from the covers and put them in a pile on the desk. He was always so tidy.

'We considered Harvey again, whether he'd had some sort of breakdown and was now re-enacting his mother's fiction. It just didn't seem likely. We even talked about you, Lily, dear. We discounted you. We doubted you'd have the necessary malice to kill someone in cold blood. None of you struck us as probable, and that was the issue. The connection wasn't there, and we didn't have enough solid evidence to suggest anyone in the group with any level of certainty. We knew we'd missed something. We'd been so focused on finding clues for the fictional murder, we had very little else to go on. So, we went to bed, and I remember making a joke about what Agatha would make of it all.'

'Agatha?' Debbie said.

'Christie,' Lily said.

'We were both tired and there was nothing more we could do before the morning. It's amazing what solutions you can come up with when you sleep on them.'

'I always say that too.' Debbie twisted her ring.

'That's nice, dear. Arthur switched off the light and slipped his hand under the cover to take hold of mine, like any other night. It's the last thing I remember before I put my hand on his chest. I didn't feel a rise and fall or a gentle beat. Half-asleep, I realised something wasn't right. I lay there for a while, listening. I woke up properly, leaned over and shook him in the dark. Thinking, as I did, he'd be cross with me for disturbing him. He was always so grumpy when woken up. I reached across and turned on the light. He should have roused. He's normally such a light sleeper. This time, he just lay there, exactly where he'd been when we'd both got into bed, his eyes wide open, fixed on nothing. I don't remember. The next thing I knew, you both arrived.'

Grace covered her face and crumpled. Debbie started pacing. She did that a lot.

'We need to take control,' Debbie said. 'Do you have a phone?'

'Yes,' Lily said. 'I told you last night. It's in the safe.'

Debbie counted off her instructions. 'I suggest we divide and conquer. I'll stay here. You retrieve your phone. We'll call the police, wake the others, and bring them up to speed. Then we can all pack while the police are on their way and get ourselves the hell out of here.'

Lily wanted to stay with Grace. She didn't understand why Debbie couldn't get her own phone and was just building up the courage to say this when Debbie pre-empted her question.

'Look, I checked my phone last night, and there wasn't any reception. The useless provider can't handle a bit of rain. Anyway, even if it's working again, there'll be a flood of notifications and messages, so it would be much easier to use yours.'

Debbie had slipped into her leadership persona and while Lily didn't appreciate being given orders, she wanted to do the right thing. Debbie might be naturally direct and a little bossy, but surely, she didn't intend to be unkind. She probably just didn't think.

Lily stroked Grace's back while she fixated on the space where the fire should be, seemingly oblivious to events going on around her.

'She'll be all right,' Debbie said, her intense need for control balanced with reassurance for once. 'I'll stay with her until you get back and it'll only take you a minute.'

Lily conceded and then remembered she'd not locked her door when she'd rushed out to see what all the screaming was about. She also wouldn't mind getting a jumper before the others congregated.

'Okay,' she said. 'Grace, I'll be back before you know it. Stay strong for me.'

She spun around and dashed upstairs, wondering why none of the others had joined them, hoping her phone would work and that Steve was awake this early to get her message.

Chapter 32

M ax flipped over in bed and reached an arm from under the covers to get his phone. He remembered where he was and that it was still locked away. He lay back again. Another terrible night's sleep. His back ached. Not surprising when you considered everything that had happened over the past couple of days. In a strange way, he was grateful it was him and not Theo who'd come on this weekend. He wondered what his old friend would have made of it. None of it fit together, and that was the problem. It was a murder mystery weekend, so a person or persons should be murdered. Or at least pretend-murdered. Feasibly, Kevin's death could be coincidence or even another red herring, and all the faff last night with the police and forensics just part of the plot. Maybe they'd all go down to breakfast and find another big reveal planned. He hoped so. He was done with all this. It definitely wasn't his scene.

Lily knew all the plot tropes. Maybe he should check his paranoia with her, get a sensible answer.

He could tell it was still early. Light crept around the edge of the blind and the clock on the side table confirmed it. That policeman had said he'd be back first thing, so he might as well get up. Max threw back the covers and let the day in. The storm had cleared, leaving only a few dark clouds lingering in the distance.

Something bugged him about the policeman too. He wasn't like the coppers who used to stop Max and his friends when they hung out on the street. The way he talked didn't ring true, and his questions were too generic. He didn't even dress the same as the community police Max sometimes spoke to over the various misdemeanours the youth centre kids committed. Still, they recruited all sorts these days and, honestly, he was past caring. As soon as they'd finished with the formalities, he was out of there. Sooner if he could. He'd worry later about who puts together a weekend where the actor playing the murderer actually dies. Not his problem.

Except he did care. Even as he dragged his empty holdall from underneath the bed and stuffed clothes into it, he kept thinking about the clues, the guests, the setting. Trying to work out in his own mind what was real and what wasn't. His heart hammered. Faster. Louder. Not good. If he didn't get himself together, he'd have another panic attack. He rested on the edge of the bed and rummaged inside the drawer of the bedside table, searching for his pills, sure he'd put them in there. He pulled the drawer out and tipped it upside down. Empty. He searched behind the table, under the bed, emptied the holdall he'd just packed, and even rummaged around the bathroom. He swore. The pills had disappeared. He sank to the floor, his back against the bed, and stared at the wall. Focus. He could do this. He didn't need those pills. Focus. He inhaled until he'd filled his lungs and kept count in his head as he released the air. Repeated. Until his heartbeat steadied and the panic subsided.

Right, he decided. No more. He was done. He'd pack, get his stuff from the safe, find Lily, and once he knew she'd be okay, he'd leave. In that order.

He stuffed his clothes back into the holdall, then punched his code into the safe and waited for it to open. It didn't, so he tried again with more force. Still nothing. He hit the flat of his palm against the top. The digital display was blank. He shifted the wardrobe away from the wall until there was a gap and peered around the back, searching to see if the power was out. The cable for the safe exited out of a hole in the wardrobe and ran straight into the wall instead of into a socket, like he'd expected. Great, he'd locked his keys in there as well. He'd need to get Elliot to sort that out, or Jamie, now he'd miraculously come back to life.

In fairness, Elliot came across as a pretty decent guy. Properly terrified of playing host, that was obvious, but he did it anyway. Max could respect that.

As for Jamie, how on earth he'd stayed still all that time when they were in the drawing room hunting for clues was beyond him. He'd managed it, though. Kudos. Demonstrated some serious concentration. Ruined the effect a bit when he'd burst into the room at dinner last night and demanded to know what was going on. He must have been watching from somewhere and that meant there must be surveillance, although Max hadn't spotted any cameras. Not important now, but he'd make sure to mention it to the police officer before he left. Pretty sure people needed permission to put cameras in places like this.

Anyway, no phone and no keys didn't need to stop him from leaving. He could just wait at the centre and get a volunteer to ring a locksmith for him. If the police weren't downstairs, he'd leave his contact details and they could come and talk to him when they were ready. Max threw the bag over his shoulder and turned his back on the room that had impressed him so much when he arrived. He stepped out into the hall.

CHAPTER 33

Lily reached the landing and pulled up short. Max was outside his room and even from here she could see the dark circles under his eyes. His clothes were crumpled, and he held the strap of his holdall slung over his shoulder, just like he had when they'd walked together from the station. That seemed a lifetime ago now. She didn't want him to leave, not without her.

He lowered the bag. 'That saves me from coming to find you,' he said.

His stance was shifty. Like he was hiding something. But then, as they kept reminding each other, everyone was hiding something, especially here.

'Are you okay?' She touched his arm.

Max pulled back. 'I'm fine. You'd better tell me what I've missed.'

'There's no easy way to say this. I'm afraid Arthur's dead.'

He recoiled like she'd punched him. His fondness for the old man had been genuine, then.

'No, that can't be right. Tell me where he is and I'll see how I can help.'

'He's in his room.' Lily studied the floor. 'By the time Debbie and I got there, he'd already gone.'

'How did you know? Why didn't you get me?' His jaw tensed.

'Grace screamed the place down. I don't know how you didn't hear, how no one except me and Debbie did.'

Another thing about this weekend that made no sense and here Max was up and dressed and ready to escape. The pills. She'd seen the bottle in his room and then seen the same bottle on Arthur's nightstand. Another coincidence, or part of the game? She couldn't keep it straight in her head. It was all getting muddled.

'There is something you could do,' she said. 'Debbie and Grace are both downstairs. I said I'd get my phone so we can chase up the police. I'm sure Grace would appreciate you sitting with her. I'd appreciate it too.' She tucked a stray piece of hair behind her ear. 'I shouldn't be long.'

'Sure thing,' he said. 'Although the power's out on my safe. The lights haven't gone out, so it can't be the main fuse. Hopefully, it's a different circuit on your side of the building, but you might need to get Elliot or Jamie to reset it.'

'Great, that's all we need.'

'Okay.' He picked up his bag. 'Here's what we'll do. I'll keep Grace company. You check if you can get your phone, and if not, I'll walk into town. I need to get out of here anyway, and I'm sure there'll be somewhere I can ring for help.'

'Sounds good,' she said. 'Thank you. I'll see you soon.'

Max walked up the stairs.

She called after him, 'And, Max?'

He turned.

'I'm glad you're here. I'm not sure who to trust anymore.'

Lily's room was exactly as she'd left it, still charming despite the unmade bed and spilled tea from when she'd fled. She bent to smooth the duvet, thinking about how neatly the covers had been tucked around Arthur. Sunrise crept through the curtains and Lily pulled them back, wanting to welcome the day and confine death to the night. Behind her character sheets, the October drizzle had returned after the heavier storms, and sunshine battled to break through the last of the clouds.

She slipped into her jeans and a woollen sweater. Max had the right idea about leaving, and she was glad he was with Grace. He'd be more comfort than Debbie would. Once she'd done the right thing by her, she wanted to leave too. Get out of this mystery house and get on with her life. The game was fun at first, but now she wasn't sure if there was a connection to the real deaths. Things had changed, and she didn't want to hang around until someone called her number. She couldn't shift a nagging doubt about those numbers. Eight had been so prominent throughout the game and now she kept attributing all sorts of things to numbers with no idea of their relevancy.

She sighed and knelt on the floor in front of the wardrobe, plugged the date of her sister's birthday into the safe and waited for the whir of the mechanism, hoping hers would work. It didn't. She tried again anyway. Still nothing. She swivelled round and sat cross-legged, like her determination would change anything. She pressed the buttons more slowly this time, but no, a blank digital display and the door stayed shut, resolutely refusing to give her back her possessions.

The room that had given her so much joy when she arrived now felt small and claustrophobic, like she was being watched – in danger, like they were all in danger. It was time to get the others together and ask some serious questions. Maybe someone had thought the same as Debbie, that the event was pretty much over and there was no need to keep their belongings locked away. She'd ask them. But first she'd get Elliot and ask him to help. He'd had a phone last night, so if she couldn't get the safe open, which apparently she couldn't, they could just use his. Then she could return to her magnolia room and her dreams. Perfect plan.

This time, she made sure she locked the door behind her. She shoved the cumbersome key into her back pocket. A tapestry of horses galloping through waves hung across where she knew the secret passage was. Six horses. She pulled it to one side and found the hidden door, then slipped into the darkened stairwell.

The bare wooden staircase creaked as she wove her way up between the framework of the house. Lily held on to the wall for guidance as she climbed the steep steps. She reached a junction, chose, and continued to climb until a white door blocked her way. The paint had peeled and the brass doorknob didn't shine like the others in the house. She twisted it and pulled, finding herself in some sort of storage area, not the living quarters she'd expected to find.

'Blast.'

She'd chosen the wrong direction and wasted precious time. As she was about to leave, rows of clear plastic boxes drew her attention. This was new and might tell her something. She edged into the room. Maybe their contents would help unravel the mystery. While the rest of the room was a black space, dusted with cobwebs, these boxes were modern and clear. She'd only be a minute.

She crept forwards in the limited light from the stairwell. The boxes were carefully lined up. They were neatly numbered and packed with items relevant to that number inside. Box five held a star; box four, a stuffed animal; three, a tripod; and so on. Box six was empty. So her theory that the clues related to the reducing number of guests was right after all, and it was part of the game, prepared long before they'd all arrived. It implied there was something connecting them, and that they were being picked off one by one, but as far as she knew, that wasn't the case. Harvey said the same thing last night. They were sure Kevin and Arthur hadn't met beforehand. In fact, none of them had, so the idea of someone gathering them all together to be murdered, fictionally or otherwise, couldn't be true. Unless. The hosts. They had all the opportunities in the world. The answers were somewhere in this attic. They must be, and she intended to find out.

Lily knelt and lifted the lid of the box closest to her. She rummaged inside. Nothing useful, just more props aligned to each number. Behind the last box, number one, with a trophy inside, was a smaller cardboard container holding a stack of photos and newspaper clippings. She pulled it out and rested it on the floor in front of her. She sat cross-legged, not caring as dust coated her jeans. Pictures of Elliot as a little boy smiled back at her. They told a story of his childhood, where a grinning child sat in an orange and brown living room on the lap of a woman with a tight perm and large plastic glasses. Next to her, a tall man with a warm face and a handlebar moustache. In front of the small family, a young girl concentrated on playing with something on the carpet, just out of view. She wasn't familiar, but there was no mistaking the boy next to her, or the dimples that had stayed with him from cute child to handsome man.

The picture quality changed with the era, as did the fashion choices of those they showed. There were birthday parties with unknown family members cheering at candles being blown out. A holiday where delighted children jumped into a swimming pool surrounded by a row of loungers, and some events that were only implied, their shots taken before they happened, where participants dressed in their finery smiled their anticipation before they'd left the house.

Lily forgot where she was, engrossed. She held each photo up to the light. The family unit stayed consistent throughout the images, while background attendees rotated. Elliot morphed from chubby child to sullen teenager to dashing man. The pictures were sorted chronologically. She paused as she held the last one up to the light. This one was of Elliot in a suit with a group of other young men and women in office clothes. The series finished. Something bothered her. She went back through, inspecting each shot. He was missing. Jamie, who had been such a fixture in Elliot's life since childhood, wasn't there. She ignored the baby snaps, kept searching until she found him. One of Elliot and a young Jamie, at a kitchen table. A young woman in an apron stood between them. Lily held the print up to the light. The woman had something familiar about her.

She moved on from the pictures to the newspaper cuttings, lifting out a bundle tied with string. A headline spoke of a child saved by a heroic policeman. The pages had faded, yellowed and smudged. Lily squinted to read the article, then heard the creak of the stairs and footsteps. She froze. Held her breath. Didn't dare to turn around as the attic door creaked shut and she was plunged into complete darkness.

CHAPTER 34

M ax sauntered in without a care in the world, his holdall slung across his back, and Debbie couldn't help but be impressed. The storm had cleared, but without access to their belongings, they were effectively trapped here, unless they fancied wandering the streets like a group of lost souls. Max didn't have the same qualms. Brave boy.

'Have you seen Lily?' she asked.

The two had become rather pally, and she'd expected the girl to be back by now, with either a phone or an Elliot.

'Yup.' He dropped the holdall on the floor by the door. 'She'll be back in a minute.' Apparently, he'd nothing else to say on the matter. He joined the group with Grace. She'd stopped crying for now, but it was clear her tears threatened to return at any moment.

Harvey prodded the logs he'd added to the fire. His perseverance paid off, and he soon got the flames burning once more. Carol clung to Grace, patting her condolences.

Grace showed incredible patience as she extracted her hand. 'Thank you, dear. I won't break. Unfortunately, when you get to my age, death isn't always unwelcome or unexpected. We knew he didn't have long.'

'What do you mean?' Debbie pulled her robe tighter. She'd need to pop upstairs to get changed soon.

The butler pushed the door open with his narrow behind. He carried a large silver tray with stacks of cups and saucers and a navy teapot. Jamie trailed behind him, still in his tweed suit and trainers. She wondered whether he'd slept in his clothes, or indeed if he'd slept at all. Not that she was one to judge. Jamie carried a silver coffee pot in one hand and a jug of milk in the other. They put the fresh drinks on the table.

'Perfect timing.' Carol wobbled over to the butler.

She was wearing those ridiculous kitten heels she couldn't balance in, for some reason. She asked for tea and the butler poured without comment, giving the impression he thought the provision of a drink acknowledgement enough. How rude. Oblivious, Carol balanced the cup and saucer, gripping it like a child carrying a precious gift, and offered it to Grace. Tea, the great healer. Grace accepted the cup and cradled it, leaving Carol holding the empty saucer.

Debbie was in no mood for tea. Someone needed to move all this along, and once again, it looked like it would fall to her to take the lead. She addressed the room.

'I've asked Lily to get her phone. When she returns, I suggest we call the police, the ambulance service and taxi company.' She paused to allow their response.

'I hope Lily's safe isn't jammed like mine is,' Harvey said.

'Mine wouldn't open either,' Max said. 'I thought it must be a fuse. Old house, things break, you know? I pulled the wardrobe out a bit. Figured I'd just swap the fuse with the one in the lamp. The cable goes straight into the wall, though, so we'll need to fix it at the source or break into it somehow.'

Debbie hummed, unimpressed. Not by Max – he'd shown more independence and capability than the rest of them put together – but by the potential lack of access to technology or money. It made her agitated, not in control. She disliked the feeling.

'The Internet's down as well,' she said. 'Or at least it was last night when I took my laptop out.'

'Have you checked this morning?' Harvey said.

'No,' she replied. 'I locked my things back up after I'd finished and I went straight to help Grace this morning.'

'Why would you lock everything away again after Kevin's death?' Harvey said.

'Force of habit. That laptop is worth a fortune and the information on it even more. It never occurred to me I wouldn't be able to access my property this morning.'

'Max must be right. It must be the fuse.' Jamie held his hands palms open, like politicians do when they are attempting to gain trust or placate someone. 'And I'm terribly sorry about the inconvenience. We'll see what we can do about returning power to the safes.'

'Good, good.' Debbie folded her arms. 'In the meantime, there must be a phone in this house somewhere.' She addressed Jamie. 'I believe you said you possess a landline. I'd like to make use of it.'

'Oh yes,' Harvey said, full of hope. 'You gave the number to the respite home.'

'It's downstairs in the servants' quarters.' Jamie turned to the butler. 'If you could escort our guest.'

The butler's gravelly voice didn't match his outfit at all. 'It's in the kitchen. I'll show you. If you'd like to follow me.'

He held the door open for Debbie, and she tried to remember whether she'd heard him speak before.

'One minute.' She crouched in front of Grace and settled her manicured hand on the frail knee of the older woman. 'We'll find out what happened, I promise.'

Debbie appraised the butler as she walked past him into the hall. There was something she didn't like about him. Her voice hardened, focused once more on the business at hand. 'Let's find this phone then,' she said, and, with her head held high, she marched out of the drawing room.

CHAPTER 35

L ily squeezed her eyes shut as if it would stop her from being discovered. She tried not to move, acutely aware of the slightest motion. Eventually, she gave in and peeked. A narrow beam of amber light swept around the attic, interrupting the darkness. As it traversed the room, it caught dust particles in the air. It would catch her, too. She fought the urge to close her eyes again. Not seeing her pursuer wouldn't help. She could hear her own heartbeat, and the floorboards creaked as the hunter skulked into the room. The beam swung around the room. It found her and it stopped. Lily held up her arm, shielded her face from the light, squinted. She couldn't make out who the person behind the light was. Whoever it was, they'd followed her up here. She had a horrible feeling she was about to die.

'What are you doing, Lily?' came a familiar London accent.

Elliot, it was Elliot. Relief washed over her. She released the breath she'd not realised she was holding. Common sense told her nothing had changed. She was still trapped in a dark attic and Elliot had as much chance, if not more, of being involved in something sinister as anyone. She just didn't believe it. It didn't matter about the box of photos of him hidden with the props. In some subconscious way, she'd already decided he wasn't the person to fear. She readied herself to reply, hoping her voice sounded stronger than she felt, maybe even a little indignant.

'I could ask you the same question.' She pushed herself up. Her limbs ached from sitting for so long. She put her hands on her hips like she was the one with the right to be there, and Elliot was the intruder.

Her arm moved through the yellow beam, pointing at the boxes. 'I think it's time you did some explaining.'

He swung the light away from her, but instead of moving it in the direction she'd pointed in, he searched the walls until he found the light switch. A bare bulb hung from the central beam. This light was warm and soft. It changed the mood of the space, made it safer somehow. Lily's fear subsided now the dusty darkness had gone. Now she knew it was Elliot. She spoke. He did the same. Speaking over each other, asking again why they were there.

Elliot yielded. 'You go.'

'What's all this?' She waved at the boxes again, expecting him to know about the contents of the attic. This was his weekend, after all.

'I've no idea. I've not been up here since we finished the renovations. It's just storage, so there's been no need.' He moved next to her.

'You honestly expect me to believe you didn't know there were props stored up here? They're clues, all arranged by number, ready to be swapped out.'

When Elliot touched her arm, Lily's goosebumps rose.

'My role was to keep the guests organised,' he said. 'The clues are static. It's the guests that make the mystery.'

Lily bit her lip. That didn't make sense.

'You already know that everyone invited here understands how mystery is constructed.'

'Yeah.'

'You all understand the mechanisms. You're all representative of the characters found in those classic stories. We simply asked you to play up some of your natural personality traits.'

'I'm not, though,' she said. 'You wouldn't exactly class me as your traditional mystery character, or Max, for that matter.'

'It's not about where you're from or what you look like, that's just modern prejudice layered over bad characterisation. You, Lily, are the perfect example of the intelligent detective the suspects trust and tell their secrets to.'

Lily studied the dusty floorboards. Her face warmed at the compliment.

Elliot sighed. 'Everything we told you about the weekend is true. We've been friends since we were at school and have wanted to start a business together as long as I can remember. Jamie's got a complicated story. Without going into the details, he was adopted and, when he was eighteen, found out all sorts about his past. It was hard for him growing up, being so different. People weren't as accepting as they are now. It never affected our friendship. Kids see past that stuff. Then when I inherited this house, it was so perfect – the stuff dreams are made of. A legacy from a distant relative of mine. Too good an opportunity to pass up and the start of an adventure. Jamie worked out all the clues to signify the number eight.'

Lily interrupted again. 'Those were misdirections, though, surely?'

'Yes,' Elliot said. 'The clues for the number eight were just a bit of fun. They never pointed to an individual. It's a game of consensus and psychology. You all had an envelope in your room and they were all the same, except one. We gave one guest extra instructions. We cast them as the murderer and their job was to avoid detection.'

'And that was Kevin?'

'It was. Neither of us wanted anyone to get hurt. Of course we didn't. This is supposed to be our opportunity to follow our dreams, and now it's all ruined. We've both put everything we've got into it. My parents invested their life savings. Now I don't know what I'm going to do.'

Lily moved closer to Elliot. Her gut instinct told her he was telling the truth. They were alike in some ways. Just people with a dream to do something better. She felt for Elliot; his dream was becoming a nightmare. Two people were dead, and it was definitely time to leave before anyone else got hurt. She focused on why she'd come up here in the first place.

'I think we should talk about all that later. I'm sorry to tell you this, but there's been another death. Arthur.'

'What?'

'I'm afraid that's not all. Everyone locked their valuables away and now our safes won't open. You had a phone last night. We need to get it, assuming you don't lock your own things away.'

'We don't. It should still be in the drawing room. Thankfully, the police are due back any minute. Let's get everyone together and I'll make another call. Make sure they're able to get through after the storm. These boxes can wait until later.'

Lily agreed. She should have told him as soon as he came in. Let the professionals work it all out.

She followed him back down the narrow stairs and into the main house. But something still wasn't sitting well with her. There was more to this, she was sure. She just couldn't quite work it out.

CHAPTER 36

The butler dawdled ahead. Debbie followed in silence, through the magnificent hallway and to the side of the main staircase, where a simple door led to the basement. She could easily have found this herself, but if he found comfort in continuing to play his part, she saw no reason to stop him, and it couldn't hurt to be escorted.

Her rational side knew it was entirely possible Arthur had died from natural causes. Grace hadn't seemed at all surprised. That's what Debbie kept telling herself, anyway. He'd been old and it could conceivably be a coincidence. It's just that she didn't believe in coincidence and that left them with somewhat of a predicament. Those incompetent boys supposedly hosting this weekend were no help whatsoever. The tweed one was clearly deluded by the great British belief that tea solves all of life's problems, and the cockney one had disappeared, probably fawning over Lily again. It seemed it would fall to her to sort things out, just like she always did.

The stairway to the basement lacked the opulence of the rest of the house. Simple, bare boards with a metal handrail. As she descended, her heels thumped, and the sound echoed. There didn't appear to be any other staff to hand, and she couldn't remember if they'd left before Kevin's death or afterwards. Regardless, that meant the solitary butler was accountable for serving the entire house. She didn't even know his name, or the protocol for dealing with a butler, or a man pretending to be a butler, at any rate. Were first names or last names more appropriate? She didn't know and wasn't sure it mattered now.

The stairs opened straight into the serving area without a single period feature. Instead, this area comprised sleek modern metal and functional appliances. No wonder they'd not shown the guests around this part of the house. It would have ruined the illusion. Florescent strip lights illuminated an island for food preparation, with a large cooking range behind, then a service space for the waiters to collect the completed dishes and carry them up to the demanding guests. To Debbie, the space itself appeared efficient and functional, while the transportation of the meals upstairs was anything but. Everything would have to be carried up the narrow staircase. While inefficiency generally irked her, there was still something to be admired in the way the architects of the original house had thought so much about the comfort of the family upstairs, and so little for those who served that family. The equal rights people today would have had a field day. She pondered whether there was a lesson in respect for hierarchy in there somewhere, even though the concept itself had fallen from favour with the current generation. Maybe something she could discuss with the team.

The butler signalled the other side of the kitchen, to another door, this one made of steel. 'The office is through there.'

'Fine,' she said, doing her best not to sound curt, while fully aware that she did. Why he couldn't have just given her directions was beyond her. She was sure she could have walked down a set of stairs and through a kitchen on her own without accompaniment. She found this strange man, who'd been half invisible until this morning, disconcerting.

She dismissed him from his duties with a flick of her hand, wanting to make the call to the emergency services in peace. He lingered, watching her. Why he, Jamie, or Elliot, for that matter, hadn't already done this was beyond her. They all seemed so submerged in this silly game and unable or unwilling to disconnect it from reality.

She fixed her work smile on her face and addressed the butler, who, for whatever reason, felt the need to supervise her progress. 'Thank you. I'll take it from here.'

Without waiting for a reply, she navigated past the service space, past the island and across to the steel door. Its weight reassured her as she heaved it open. The automatic lights flickered on. The office was perfectly square, unusual for a house this old. High on the far wall, steel bars covered a rectangle of window. A filing cabinet nestled in the corner with a leafy plant in an ugly pot on top. In front of it, a cheap modern desk curved on one side to allow the faux-leather executive chair to be pulled in tight towards it. The budget furniture and fittings were at least offset by a generous investment in their technology. A high spec, flat-screen computer with a Bluetooth mouse and keyboard, all an expensive brand she recognised. The only nod to the history of the house was the beige rotary telephone on the desk.

Debbie settled herself in the chair and reached over to pick up the handset. She peered at the dial and slotted her manicured index finger into the space for the nine, ready to bring it round three times. She hadn't known they even made phones like this anymore. When she cradled the handset in her neck, it evoked nostalgia for a time gone by. She was someone more used to wireless earbuds.

The phone was silent. She drummed the receiver, knowing full well it wouldn't revive the ringtone. She spun the chair to face the door, ready to demand more answers from the butler, even though she didn't expect him to be there after she'd sent him away. Now she'd need to find him, or those host boys. She let out a frustrated groan. A sharp pain on the back of her head. The phone clattered to the ground. Debbie tried to raise her hand. To touch the place where it hurt. By the time her hand was halfway there, she'd started to slide to the ground. How annoying. She'd never find out if she'd won the competition.

Chapter 37

M ax regretted his promise to Lily. There were plenty of other people fussing around Grace and he could be more useful doing something else, anything else, just as long as it didn't involve this house. He wanted to leave and didn't understand why they couldn't just walk into town and stop pretending like they were completely cut off from the world. No storm could be so bad. Not in this country. There might be a couple of fallen trees, the odd bin in the street; nothing insurmountable.

The promised police officer still hadn't shown up, and Lily was taking longer than he'd thought she would. Max glanced at the clock on the mantelpiece and silently calculated how long it would take him to get home if he left now.

Lily slid into the room, Elliot following close behind. Max gave her an expectant stare, wondering whether she'd been successful with her telephone mission. She shook her head and went to check on Grace. She knelt in front of her, gazing up at the woman's face. Grace fought her tears valiantly, although her face wore the shock of grief, like a new and unwanted outfit. Max knew that feeling all too well. He hated that he wasn't strong enough to comfort others yet. He still needed to work through his own pain. Lily spoke to Grace. Her voice was louder than he'd heard her speak before, and what she said seemed intended for everyone.

'I think we should get you home.' She twisted to face Jamie and Elliot. 'I know the police asked us to stay, but circumstances have changed, and I think it would be best if we left.'

Elliot stayed silent.

'I agree,' Max said. 'This is too much. You've got our addresses, and it's not like we're going to run off anywhere. Even if Debbie got through to the police, it's time to go. She's been a long time.'

Jamie edged his foot back, shifted his weight, blocking his way, or preparing for a fight. Either way, Max was done.

'This is ridiculous,' Max said. 'It's not like we're in the middle of nowhere. It can't be more than two miles walk to the station. I can be there and back in less than an hour if some of you want to wait here. There's no reason for us to stay in this room like we're waiting for a brilliant detective to come in and give us the big reveal. This isn't a novel, and it's time to stop acting like it is.'

He wasn't the first person to say that, he knew, but this time, he wasn't asking for permission. He marched out of the room, ignoring the others. When he reached the front door, he slid the flimsy security chain across and pulled the handle. Locked. He lifted the catch and pulled, then pulled again with more force, like that would make a difference. He needed the key. The obvious place for it to be was in one of the cabinet drawers. He yanked them open. No key, only some scraps of paperwork and a bottle of crimson stain, a leftover prop from Jamie's 'murder'. That felt like a world away.

Determined, he pivoted, marching back through the hall and towards the conservatory, reasoning that while they might well lock the front door securely at night, it was possible the back was less fastidiously treated. He'd always nagged Theo for forgetting to lock the back door in the summer. Theo used to laugh and say if people were determined enough to climb through an overgrown alley, over a six-foot wall and into his yard to rob him of his meagre possessions, they probably needed them more than he did and were welcome to them. When Max had moved in, he double-checked the lock every night before he went to bed.

In the conservatory, a red and orange dawn marked the end of the night. The half-light cast strange silhouettes on empty tables, patiently waiting for their diners. He tried the conservatory door. Also locked. He swore, grabbed a chair and hurled it against the window. He panted. The chair bounced back at him from the re-enforced panes. Pivoting again, ready to search out another option, maybe go down to the basement, maybe find a servants' entrance, see what the hell had happened to Debbie. He'd break the house to pieces if necessary. Break their hosts until they gave up the key. With his back to the conservatory door, he collided with Harvey, who'd appeared from nowhere. He recoiled, searched the shadows, focused on what hid in the dark. Max couldn't make out his face, only the hollows where his eyes should be and his small, white-toothed smile.

Max held up his palm and demanded, 'Why are you following me?' Then, more rationally, 'And how did you get in here without me noticing?'

Harvey moved into the light and held his plump finger to his lips, this time calm. 'Sit down a minute, for pity's sake, and I'll tell you what I know. I think it's clear where the plot is heading and we need to re-write the ending, or none of us will leave alive.'

His voice might have been calm, but his words sounded deranged. Still talking like this was part book, part game. Max knew his expression gave away his scepticism.

Harvey shook his head. 'It's not me. Think about it. All of us are interested in, or have a connection to, crime novels. That makes sense, but what else do we have in common?'

He lifted a chair and took a seat, then gestured for Max to join him. They must have looked ridiculous, like they were waiting for breakfast to be served. Max's curiosity spiked.

He righted the fallen chair and leaned forwards on his elbows. 'Okay, I'm listening. Tell me what you've got.'

'It's all a matter of plot and character archetypes. Eight guests invited to a murder mystery weekend. That equals eight suspects and eight potential victims. We know there's something other than simply liking to read that connects us, so we need to pool our resources to work out what that thing is, or right now, I'd say there's a high probability none of us will survive.'

A touch over-dramatic, although he did have a point.

'Okay, I'm with you, but, no offence, you and I don't have anything in common,' Max said. 'You live in the suburbs, I live in the city, you're a full-time carer while I'm an artist and youth centre worker, and let's be honest, we couldn't look more different.'

'It might not be what we do or who we are. It could be something we've done. A crime that deserves retribution or revenge for a broken heart.'

Now he'd got Max's attention. Max wanted to know more about this heart-breaking, criminal Harvey; however, he was still talking, listing off the key reasons one person might want to kill another and oblivious to Max trying to block out the babbling to concentrate on the facts hidden within.

Harvey eventually reached the end of his list of motives, but he wasn't done. He took a deep breath and carried on, changing tack. 'Let's imagine for a moment that Kevin and Arthur were the only targets. I don't believe that for a second, but it will make it easier to think through. Let's start with them. What links a cantankerous miser with a charming, retired police officer?'

Nothing sprang to mind.

'No,' Max said. 'That's not it. We're assuming it's the guests linked to each other, but it's not. What if there really is no connection between you and me at all, apart from reading mystery novels?'

'Okay, I'm with you,' Harvey said. 'I still can't think what injustice I've committed that would make someone want to kill me, can you?'

'No, and I also can't fathom a connection between Kevin and Arthur.'

Max folded his arms. 'I'm with you, too. There's someone here with a link to everyone else. Not a collective link in the sense they've all cheated on their partners or they've all stolen something. You think it's an individual act committed by each of them, of us, towards a single person.'

'Yes.' Harvey pinched his bottom lip. 'We need to work through the options. That police officer said he'd be back today. I'm not so sure, though. I don't think we should wait any longer. And I think we'd be safest all together so no one else can get hurt. We either need to contact the outside world or get ourselves out there.'

Max stood and patted Harvey's shoulder. 'You might use a lot of words to get there, you know, but you speak a lot of sense. Let's hope Debbie got through on the phone and all this is unnecessary.'

'Absolutely, there's always hope.'

The strange crime partnership moved out of the conservatory and back into the hall. Somewhere in the depths of the house, a clock struck five.

CHAPTER 38

To Lily's relief, whatever Harvey had said to Max had settled him down. His jaw had loosened, and he'd relaxed a little. Good. On the floor next to Grace, Lily tucked her feet under herself. Grace's hands shook as she clasped them together above the blanket. Her elegant glamour had evaporated along with the life of the man she'd loved for decades.

Max fumbled with an apology. 'Sorry if I came across a bit frantic just then.' He tucked his thumbs into his jean pockets. 'I don't like being locked in.'

Harvey made his way towards his favoured armchair by the fire. He cleared his throat, and the others, for once, gave him their undivided attention. They wanted answers, and however slim the chance that Harvey would provide them, they were ready to take that chance. Maybe he'd emerge as the brilliant detective. For the first time that weekend, he spoke with precision and gravitas.

'We need to accept this is no longer a game.' He gripped the arms of the chair like they were giving him strength. 'We're locked in the house. One of us is a murderer, and I'd have thought by now you've all worked out the police aren't coming. That leaves us with one option. To stick together, work out who the culprit is, restrain them, and then break our way out.'

Lily observed the extraordinary change in how the guests responded to him. They'd transitioned from completely disregarding Harvey's charming chatter to listening to him as if he were some sort of oracle. Jamie leaned against the wall nonchalantly, as he, too, listened to Harvey. She wondered what he made of him.

'At the risk of asking a silly question, why can't we just walk out of the front door?' Carol said.

'That's not a silly question at all. It's an excellent question.' Harvey rewarded his sidekick with an appreciative smile. 'It's locked and we'll get into that in a minute. First, I think Elliot has something to say about the setup of the weekend.'

Elliot lost the rigid stance of his country gentleman persona. It must have been exhausting pretending to be someone he wasn't for so long. Now, his shoulders slumped forwards, his neck elongated by the change in posture. He moved around the desk and perched on the edge. 'I swear to you all, this wasn't part of the plan,' he said. 'The mystery was supposed to be solved last night. You all worked out there was a connection to the number eight. What you don't know is that we selected the murderer at random, based purely on your allocated rooms. When you arrived, you signed the guest book, and I picked a key from the drawer. The keys were just sitting loose, so the room I showed you to was nothing more than chance. All the rooms had an envelope in them to give you some background about the house, me and Jamie, and about the game. One envelope also contained an extra piece of paper in it asking the guest to play the role of murderer. We'd prepared the envelopes in advance, shuffled them up and then given them to the staff to put in the rooms. We didn't want to know who the culprit was, in case we gave it away by mistake.'

Lily watched the others as they mulled over Elliot's words, testing them to see if they believed him. She had some thoughts of her own and while she formed those thoughts into sentences, Harvey again stepped up, metaphorically at least. It seemed he intended to stay in that chair for the foreseeable future.

'That makes sense,' he said. 'It's a game of psychology as much as it is prob-lem-solving.'

Carol caught on. 'So, no one knew Kevin got the extra instructions except for Kevin himself. That might explain why he was so difficult to get along with, although I tend to think there was a large dash of his actual personality involved in that, too. It sort of explains Kevin's nature, but it doesn't explain why he or Arthur died.'

Grace whimpered at her husband's name, but kept her composure.

Harvey rubbed the side of his face. 'There's more. There must be. Something that will open up the mind of the murderer to us.'

Lily found her voice again. 'There is more,' she said. 'Elliot, it's time to tell them what we found.'

Elliot clenched his fists. 'Yes. You're right, of course. Lily and I did find something else, and it wasn't part of the original plan. Up in the attic, there's a storage room. I'd not been up there since we renovated the house. There's been no need. It was empty, as far as I was concerned. Lily was looking for me and took the stairs to the storage space instead of the old bedrooms. I heard someone in there and went to investigate. It's filled with boxes of props all relevant to specific numbers.'

This time Carol's face stayed blank, and Harvey picked up the thread. 'So, that explains why we saw references to the number eight changing to seven and then to six. It confirms this is definitely not a coincidence, and these deaths were premeditated. These murders. It means the killer had access to the attic, prior knowledge of the theme, as well as a motive. Please remember, the purpose of a whodunnit isn't really to work out who, it's to work out why.'

Harvey, secure in his role as amateur detective, stood, clasped his hands behind his back and walked from one person to the next. Lily already knew what he was about to say and was grateful it didn't fall to her to vocalise it.

'Which one of us has a connection to the others?' he said. 'Who believes they were wronged and is so broken they would kill for it?'

He moved between the guests, scrutinising their expressions for answers she wasn't sure he'd find. Past Carol, Max and Grace. Then drew his conclusion and stopped in front of the hosts.

'None of us had access to the attic to prepare the clues, so it's not a guest. And it's not Elliot.' He faced Jamie. 'I think you have some explaining to do.'

CHAPTER 39

J amie removed his hands from his pockets and gave a slow, mocking round of applause. 'Congratulations, big man. You finally worked it out. Well. Some of it. Got the who...'

He stopped mid-clap and pulled a disappointed face. 'But you still need the why and the how. That amateur hack of a mother only taught you plot tropes. Didn't actually teach you how to think it through.'

Max shifted in front of Lily, arms by his side, ready to protect her if need be. How gallant, not that Jamie was interested in them yet. For now, he focused on Harvey, who, now he'd shared his revelation, didn't seem to know what to do next. He twisted his hands in front of himself, his neck a mottled pink. Jamie couldn't care less. He'd spent enough time pretending, and now he could finally focus on him. Grace whimpered. She muttered Arthur's name almost inaudibly and rocked as her grief took over.

Jamie's attention swung in her direction. 'Oh, and your majestic husband. Who would've thought the brains behind his perceived brilliance came not from the acclaimed constable, but from a withered old hag? All those years, you let him take the credit for your ideas as long as he did what you directed. He was your puppet and damn the repercussions.'

To Jamie's surprise, Grace surged from her chair. She spat her fury at him as she spoke. 'You don't know what you're talking about, you vicious little man. My husband and I were a team. He was the kindest, most generous person

I've ever met. What could he possibly have done to you that could warrant murdering him? We've never even met you before this weekend.'

Jamie indulged her little outburst. He could see the confusion of his captives over the top of the old lady's silver hair. He wanted them to die. Harvey, to give him credit, was right about another important thing. He also wanted them to know why. Apparently, there would be a big reveal after all.

'Take a seat, old lady. I'll admit, I'm disappointed,' he said. 'As none of you can work it out yourselves, I'd better let you in on my secrets and explain why you all deserve a place at my weekend retreat.'

No one moved. He expected compliance, no, demanded it.

He spoke with more force. 'Sit down, now. All of you.'

They did. Harvey lowered himself back into his armchair, Grace on the sofa with Lily huddled next to her. Carol and Max also chose armchairs, which left Elliot, who'd stayed silent throughout all of this with a bemused expression on his face.

'You too,' Jamie said.

Elliot complied. Marvellous. They sat like a dysfunctional family in front of the fireplace, where Jamie waited until the perfect amount of confusion had settled onto the faces of his guests.

'Why?' Elliot, the most confused of all, sounded as pathetic as he looked.

'Yes, we'll get to that.' Jamie waved away the comment. He was in no mood to listen to any more of Elliot's constant whining.

'The police will be here any minute.' Carol's voice shook as she spoke.

Jamie snorted. 'Really?'

She shrank back into herself.

The butler strode through the now amenable guests and stood by Jamie's side. He acknowledged him briefly, then returned his attention to his guests, marvelling at his accomplishment. Everyone that had ever caused him pain. He'd brought them all together. And he'd let them wait just a short while longer, enjoy his power as they all tried to work out what they had in common, what they'd done to warrant being here, and whether they could escape. Jamie glanced at Elliot, who was now studying the floor in a way that was reminiscent of Lily. They'd have made a lovely couple in a different life. Somehow, it was fitting they would never get the chance. Elliot had enjoyed a lifetime of getting all the chances. It was only fair. The clock ticked in the background.

A movement at the edge of Jamie's vision.

Max lunged towards him.

CHAPTER 40

Lily watched in horror as Max flew across the room at Jamie. No noise. No cry of attack. Just one man, intent on taking down another. Lily recoiled. Max's arms stretched towards Jamie. He didn't make it. Instead, he dropped to the ground mid-flight like someone had switched on gravity. Jamie shifted, ever so subtly, and drew a gun.

Jamie pointed the gun at Max's forehead with a steady hand and carefully spoken words. 'I don't think so.'

The ultimate challenge. Jamie clicked a bullet into the cylinder. This was it, then. He wanted them all dead. No one was coming to save them.

Max stared past the gun, straight at Jamie. No hint of fear as the two men locked eyes, considered their next move. He squared his shoulders and presented his challenge. 'You going to shoot me here in front of an audience? Doesn't sound like your style.'

Jamie's lip curled. 'So brave, but not so quick, are you, Isaac?'

Jamie lingered on the name. Lily had forgotten Max was a nickname. It felt like forever ago when he'd asked to be called that. Whatever reaction Jamie expected, Max didn't oblige. He considered his next move with bravery and complete composure.

Jamie tipped the old-fashioned revolver from one hand to the next as though testing its weight. 'There are six bullets in this gun,' he said, 'one for each of you.'

He swung the barrel from guest to guest and finally landed at Elliot.

They'd all been so keen to hear the big revelation, and now it had arrived. A room of guests on a murder mystery weekend and a single culprit who'd planned his vengeance for reasons still unknown. Jamie directed the gun at Max while his gaze moved to Elliot. His best friend supposedly, his partner. Elliot's face wore a mixture of bewilderment and hurt. Like he was trying to work out what to say, and couldn't find the words.

Max didn't waste any time. He lunged forwards again. Jamie stumbled, knocked off balance, but still upright. The gun fired. Max howled as the bullet found its target. He collapsed. There should have been blood. For a while, there was none. Max lay crumpled on the ground. Lily rushed to his side, and then the blood came. It pooled around Max on the floor. His face paled and his eyes rolled back. Lily picked up his hand and held it against her chest. She screamed.

Lily forced herself to stop. Silence. Her mind raced to search out anything she could do for Max. Nothing. There was nothing she could do, or any of the rest of them. He'd given so much and showed such bravery.

She couldn't help but draw parallels with the last time she'd seen a body on the drawing room floor. Jamie had lain there for hours, pretending to be dead. Lily wished this were the same, while the last glimmer of hope faded away with her friend.

The last clues clicked into place, the connections, all the strange goings-on in Kendrick Manor, and now it seemed so obvious that Jamie was behind it all. She didn't know it all, but she knew enough, and she didn't want to die. Not today. She clutched Max's hand to her chest as if she could somehow transfer some of her life into him, and just maybe absorb some of his fearlessness back into herself.

She tried to keep the terror from her voice as she confronted Jamie. Maybe they could still talk their way out of this.

'I know about you,' she said. 'You're not as clever as you think you are.'

'Oh yes, and what is it you think you know?' Jamie said.

'More than you'd expect. I've seen the newspaper clippings in the attic. I know Kevin was your father and Arthur was the policeman who took you away when you were little.'

'Well done.' He sneered.

Lily desperately needed help, but Carol, Harvey and Grace all stayed frozen on the spot. With Elliot's theatrical host persona long gone, he, too, stayed silent. Shell-shocked. She needed Elliot to back up what she'd said.

When he did, he spoke in hardly more than a whisper. 'We found the boxes in the attic.'

Lily had mistakenly assumed he'd been too preoccupied with the pictures of himself to realise the significance; it would have been a bigger leap for him to make, after a lifetime of experiences reinforcing his view of the goodness in Jamie, and none of the monster it was becoming clear he was.

Now she thought about it. There'd been a slight resemblance between Jamie and Kevin. Subtle. You'd never have noticed if you'd not been told.

Jamie scoffed. 'Well done. It appears our little mouse detective and her assistant are smarter than I gave you credit for. Kevin should have loved me, but he got a better offer and just threw us aside. Mother didn't want me without him. I should have been one of the lucky ones, getting adopted, but women can't be trusted. Mummy number two ran off and Dad did the right thing and sought help.' He turned his venom and his gun towards Carol. 'You were supposed to care for me when my father couldn't. Take the place of a mother. Instead, you gave all your affection to the others, your favourites. No matter what I did to get your attention.'

Harvey's mouth opened and closed like he wanted to speak, but all the words had stuck. Carol's chest heaved. She raised her hand and dragged back the blonde wig she'd been patting back into place all weekend. Beneath, she'd hidden her real hair beneath a fine mesh to keep it in place. She pulled that off too, letting her silver-flecked hair fall to her shoulders in untidy waves.

'It can't be,' she said. 'James. It's been years. Why are you doing this and what are you talking about?'

'And why are you wearing a wig?' Harvey said.

'Questions, questions.' Jamie waved the gun. 'Let's start at the top.' He paused to make sure they were all listening. 'You're all here for a reason. Kevin was first on the list, and getting him here was so wonderfully simple. All I needed to do was to intercept the daily newspaper and replace it with one I'd doctored. The paper delivery brat was all too willing to help in exchange for a pitifully small amount of money. Who says teenagers are mercenary? Anyway, I scattered indicators in the crossword puzzles Kevin enjoyed so much and was so terrible at completing. They enticed him to apply to attend the mystery weekend, gradually getting easier, so he'd think he was improving and was in with a chance.

'Then I placed the adverts. Not every day. I didn't want it to be too obvious, just often enough, so when he'd thought about the clues, combined with the ads, he'd consider entering. A bit of psychology and a few well-timed leaflets added to the effect. Then, the master stroke, the competition crossword. I suggested it was not only cryptic but virtually impossible, so only the most skilled would be capable of completing it and could enter the competition to win the weekend. He fell for it and rang a few days later.

'I'll admit there were a few times I thought I'd messed it up, it shouldn't have been that hard, the clues were all recycled from previous weeks, but then he never was the smartest man, as we can deduce from some of his life choices.'

Jamie's lip twisted into an evil smile. He held the gun, like he was directing an orchestra.

Harvey found his voice again. 'If Kevin was your father, that still doesn't explain why you brought the rest of us here, or why Carol is in disguise.'

'Quite simple. I just couldn't bear to look at her. She was always so prim and precise, with that perfect family of hers, taking in the waifs and strays.' He glared at Lily. 'I can't believe the penny hasn't dropped. That summer you spent with us, the stuck-up bookworm, too clever to play with the other children.'

'I always did the best for the children in my charge.' Carol twisted the hairnet in her hands. 'You were troubled, picked on the others, kept breaking things.'

Lily drew in a breath. 'I remember you. Mrs Dickinson. I played at your house after school. The summer my mum was ill.'

'You did.' Carol gave her a fond smile. 'You were such a bonny little girl. I hardly recognise you all grown up, such a beauty and so clever. Your parents must be proud of you.'

'You see,' Jamie said. 'Favourites.'

Lily couldn't believe he'd kept up this deception for so long. He'd been friends with Elliot for over thirty years, and yet, this evil side of him must have been there all along, waiting for a trigger.

Carol picked at the bridge of her nose. 'Prosthetic,' she said.

When she'd finished peeling away her disguise, her features were completely different, not better or worse, but different for sure. The face of Lily's childminder all those years ago. Jamie pointed the gun at her and clicked the next bullet into the barrel.

'Pathetic.' He strolled a few steps back and forth along the length of the hearth and waved the gun. It appeared to be more for dramatic purposes than because he was intending to fire. She hoped she was right.

'Daddy Kevin was pathetic, too. What a stupid man, not just for deserting us in the first place, but for standing by that mistake. You were both so easy to manipulate. A few crossword puzzles and the odd suggestion dotted around. Enticing you with the promise of helping your son's friend was a master stroke, if I do say so myself. I'll admit, I enjoyed learning about prosthetics though, Rebecca.'

So, Carol was really Rebecca, and she'd been their childminder. Kevin was Jamie's biological father, the one who'd left him when he was a baby for another woman, and Arthur was the police officer that took him away. That still didn't give any motive for why she, Max, or Harvey were there. She expected they'd get to that.

Tears welled in Carol's eyes. 'You. You set this all up, you made me believe I was helping my son, you made me dress up like this and change my name. Then you killed Kevin and Arthur. You always were a spiteful child. I did my best. What's wrong with you?'

'Nothing at all, quite the opposite. I just wanted to redress the balance, and it was so much fun. Watching you suffer as all your unhappiness and uncertainty came to the surface. I considered putting you in Manderley, but decided it would be too obvious. All things considered, it felt more appropriate for the little mouse.'

Carol crumpled in her seat.

Lily still held on to Max's hand. The longer they could keep Jamie talking, the more chance there was they could talk him down, or come up with some other plan to get out of there.

'What about the rest of us?' she asked. 'What about me, Max, Debbie? And where is Debbie? She must have found the phone by now.'

Even as she said it, she knew she wasn't coming back. Neither the police nor anyone else was on their way to save them.

The tall figure of the butler moved from the edge of the room and stood shoulder to shoulder with Jamie. 'Might as well tell them the rest,' he said.

Chapter 41

J amie turned appreciatively to the butler. He'd done well, and Jamie agreed: this was the perfect time to tell them all what was coming next. Lily closed her eyes like she was praying. Praying none of this was happening, or that she could disappear. He didn't care. They were all pathetic. They'd come along so willingly and done exactly what he'd wanted them to do. Almost a disappointment. Almost too easy.

Elliot crouched by Lily's side and took her hand in his, gently pulling her away from Max. Such consolation for the little mouse. How sweet. Overall, he reflected, things were progressing nicely. The guests had all acted more or less as he'd expected them to. Yes, there'd been a few minor twists in the plot. He hadn't predicted Lily would go snooping in the attic, for example. Nothing he couldn't handle, though, and now here was Elliot, literally on the floor at his feet. Where he belonged.

To be fair, he hadn't predicted their budding romance either. What fun he could have had with that, if he'd known they'd develop a crush on each other. He couldn't remember the last time Elliot had had a girlfriend, and it was such an interesting twist that he not only liked Lily, but that she returned those affections. Oh well, another time, another place maybe. A tad nauseating to be honest, although, in its own way, gratifying that they'd found each other just before they were both going to die.

Elliot had been the easiest of all to manipulate. He never questioned where the props for the house came from, never suspected when Jamie went off on his research expeditions. The whole setup had been his idea, and he'd been so grateful anyone believed in him that, once they did, he noticed nothing else.

It hadn't always been like that. Jamie genuinely was thankful that Elliot had offered him friendship when they'd been children. Time chipped away at them, though, and once they were teenagers, Jamie had realised he liked Elliot's money and unquestioning obedience far more than he did the boy himself. He was so clingy. At least this would be the last time Jamie had to put up with him.

The pool of blood around Max crept across the rug. Annoying. Jamie rather liked that rug. Elliot crouched at a strange angle, restricted by the ridiculous suit he insisted on wearing.

Jamie wielded the gun, expertly, he thought, swinging it around the room. 'Where to begin?' He stopped the gun when it landed on Carol, still finding it difficult to reconcile her with the Mrs Dickinson of his childhood. 'You always blathered on about your perfect son, made the rest of us feel so insignificant. Funny, I was terrified of you as a child, not so much anymore.'

Carol stuttered. 'I did my best.' Pathetic tears fell down her face. 'Your father told me you needed a firm hand. I couldn't let you bully the other children. You were clearly troubled.'

'I wasn't the bully, you were.' Jamie spat his words in her face. 'I can't believe how afraid you made me. Look at you now. Bedraggled and broken, waiting for your just deserts.'

Carol's hands shook as she clasped them on her lap. Months he'd spent listening to her drone on about her son and how much she wanted to help him. He still couldn't believe she hadn't recognised him or that she'd been so amenable to covering her face in plastic and wearing a wig to go undercover. A dash of misdirection was all it took to stop Lily from recognising her.

'I know I was only there one summer,' Lily said. 'But I don't remember any unkindness.'

'Of course you don't, perfect Lily, huddled in the corner with a book while the rest of us were punished for playing.'

'You were too rough.' Carol quivered. 'The other children were afraid of you. I asked your father to help, and he told me what to do.'

Jamie waved the gun. 'My father was a strong and brilliant man. You. Are nothing.'

He sucked in a breath. A few more hours and it would all be over. He'd lock up the manor and leave them all dead inside. He wondered how long it would be until someone found their bodies. Someone was bound to come searching for the missing policeman, eventually. The storm last night added a certain ambience to the weekend that he appreciated, but the actor getting stuck here because of it was a bit of an inconvenience. Still, they'd locked him safely in the cupboard and one more wouldn't make much difference. By the time anyone did come looking, Jamie would have jetted off somewhere sunny, leaving behind the perfect murder and the perfect scapegoat. The fire warmed his back and Jamie undid the top button of his shirt. He might burn this tweed monstrosity, too.

Harvey muttered away to himself. He tapped the armrest like he was hoping to alert help with some sort of fat-person Morse code. Jamie debated. Maybe he'd shoot Harvey next, at least it would shut him up.

'Well?' he asked. 'Something on your mind?'

'I think—' Harvey said, but Elliot launched himself from the floor, letting out a pathetic battle cry. Clever Elliot, doing the unexpected for once. Jamie stepped back. Elliot reached for the gun rather than the man and it went off again. A bullet hit the wall as the gun flew from Jamie's grasp. It spun on the surface of the cabinet as it landed and dropped behind it.

'What the hell do you think you're doing?' Jamie shoved Elliot out of the way, back to the floor where he belonged.

Elliot landed with a satisfying thud. Jamie dropped to his knees and stretched his arm underneath the furniture to reach for the revolver, but the space was too small.

He punched the butler's arm. 'Get the gun, then.'

Chapter 42Lily couldn't believe she'd missed it. The butler had been part of the whole thing. Of course. That explained how props moved position around the manor with no one noticing. Lily tried to be rational. She could hardly have expected herself to anticipate there was not one but two deluded killers in the manor, and quite frankly, she could worry about working out plot points later. For now, there were two priorities: getting away from their tormentors and finding a way out of the house.

Elliot's hair fell across his face as he pushed himself up. She felt torn between comforting him and staying with Max. The clock ticked, and the fire crackled, both accompaniment to Lily's thumping heart. Grace rocked in her chair and Carol fidgeted, even more uncomfortable now she was out of disguise. Harvey, the least likely of all of them to act, and yet, the one who did.

He sprang from his chair and, in a fluid motion, yanked the edge of the lace tablecloth from the cabinet, sweeping it off like an amateur magician. Such a small cloth. Ridiculous really, but when he threw it over Jamie, it was enough to confuse him as he swiped at it. Harvey grabbed the hardback chair from underneath Carol as she stood, or Rebecca, or whatever her name was now. He held the legs forwards to shepherd the butler into the corner of the room.

'Time for us to leave,' he called back, and the others didn't need to be asked twice. Elliot offered his hand to Lily. A fleeting moment of concern and care before they tumbled out of the room. Carol wobbled to her feet and offered Grace a similar shelter, only to be batted away. Grace straightened her shoulders, her face fixed with pure determination.

Neither Elliot nor Harvey had bought them much time, just a few precious seconds, and that was all they needed to get out of the drawing room and into the hall. Harvey went last, edging backwards with the chair legs held high. As he passed through the door into the hall, Elliot was ready, and pushed it closed behind him. Then the two men wedged the back of the chair under the handle in the hope it would delay Jamie and the butler.

'Let's go to the attic,' Elliot said. 'I've got copies of all the keys up there and one of the old servants' rooms set up as a kind of control centre. There are cameras hooked up throughout the house and the feed goes straight to my laptop.'

Grace gave him a disapproving stare, but unless Lily was mistaken, her sparkle was coming back. 'Let's forget for a minute that you've been spying on us. You have keys, a computer and the Internet. That's it. That's our way out of here.'

Moving from one enclosed space to another with a madman on your heels struck Lily as a foolish thing to do. She'd seen enough horror films over the years. Her mind searched for an alternative, but on this occasion, it did seem the best option. They couldn't break out, so without a key they were trapped and at least this way they'd be together, they could close the hidden door behind them and the cameras meant they'd be able to keep tabs on what Jamie and the butler were up to while they waited for rescue.

The others didn't show any such concerns. Elliot pushed the wooden panel and lifted the tapestry to uncover the hidden entrance. The guests filed behind him, squeezing up the narrow staircase towards the servants' quarters. When they reached the landing on the first floor, Elliot took the opposite way to the one Lily had taken earlier.

Lily peeked at Harvey. He ascended backwards, using the back of his heel to feel for the next step, his body protecting the others in case anyone followed. The crashing sounds from the drawing room quietened the further up they climbed. Lily knew a chair propped under a door handle wouldn't hold them inside for long. They'd simply rip the tape from the double doors and leave via the dining room. Their pursuers wouldn't be far behind.

The attic room Elliot so grandly called the 'control centre' was too small for five adults to fit into comfortably. Lily slipped into the space under the eaves, tucked up on the floor with her knees to her chest, her arms wrapped around them.

Elliot reached down to pull a laptop from underneath the chair. Not so in control now. Grace settled in the other chair. Carol stood awkwardly behind. There was no way Harvey was going to fit, so he became the unofficial doorway guard.

Flat screens mounted on the wall showed images of the house. The drawing room displayed on the middle and largest screen. Jamie and the butler were still in there. The lace cloth lay crumpled on the floor, surrounded by broken ornaments. They were inching the large cabinet away from the wall, edging it little by little, until they created enough space to manoeuvre behind it and retrieve the gun. The butler had removed his tailcoat. His face contorted as he slipped his arm into the gap.

Other screens showed the communal spaces. The dining room had been laid as if it were expecting guests to arrive, with places set and fresh candles waiting to be lit. No disturbance at all from Kevin's demise the night before. The conservatory, where the tables were bare, all lined up uniformly except for two chairs pulled out of place. Warm light bathed the majestic hallway, ready to welcome visitors. A smaller screen showed a rotating image of the working rooms. The office, the pantry and the kitchen.

'It's so we could coordinate mealtimes,' Elliot said. 'Make sure preparations were on track, that sort of thing. We needed to make sure guests weren't using a room we needed to set up.' It made sense. But something looked wrong.

Lily squinted at the image. 'Can you make it stay on the office, please? I think that's Debbie. It's too small to see. Is she okay?'

Elliot slid his fingertip across the pad and enlarged the image. Lily leaned forwards. She was right. It was Debbie. The once vivacious and frankly terrifying woman was now slumped across the desk. Like she'd fallen asleep working, except the angles were all wrong. They should get to her, find out if they could help her. None of them should be alone in the manor.

Elliot must have thought the same. 'I hate to sound callous, but checking on her will have to wait. There's nothing we can do for her now.'

Grace interrupted. 'All right, dear, enough of all this dallying. We need to get out of here. Being trapped in a small room where the only way out is a narrow staircase hasn't exactly improved our odds.' She pointed to the laptop. 'Will that thing connect to the Internet?'

Elliot tapped the keys. He hit them more and more vigorously, so clearly it wouldn't.

Lily unwrapped her arms from her knees. 'Whatever his reasons for wanting to kill us, Jamie set this whole thing up as a tribute to the great mysteries of all time, so we need to think like the famous detectives from the books we all love.' She implored Harvey. 'What would Mary Bakewell do?'

Harvey rubbed the side of his face. He took a deep breath before he spoke. 'In a novel, the detective would talk the killer down. They would regret their ways, make their confession, and leave peacefully with the police. I don't think any of us fancy trying to coax Jamie out of his plan, and there's no sign of the police.'

Grace slid from the chair and reached under the small coffee table in the corner. When she sat up, she held a long white cable covered in dust.

'Let's start by sorting out this laptop.' She reclaimed her chair and reached her other hand forwards to Elliot, showing she'd like him to pass her the laptop, which he did without a word. Grace fixed the Ethernet cable into the connection on the side and smoothed her fingers along the keys, familiarising herself with it.

She smiled at the shocked faces around her. 'Just because I was a housewife doesn't mean that's all I've ever done. I'm rather skilled at coding, so setting up an Internet connection shouldn't be too much of a challenge.'

Elliot tried unsuccessfully to hide his astonishment.

'I'll deal with this, dear. You find those keys.'

The image of Jamie and the butler in the drawing room shattered.

CHAPTER 42

Lily couldn't believe she'd missed it. The butler had been part of the whole thing. Of course. That explained how props moved position around the manor with no one noticing. Lily tried to be rational. She could hardly have expected herself to anticipate there was not one but two deluded killers in the manor, and quite frankly, she could worry about working out plot points later. For now, there were two priorities: getting away from their tormentors and finding a way out of the house.

Elliot's hair fell across his face as he pushed himself up. She felt torn between comforting him and staying with Max. The clock ticked, and the fire crackled, both accompaniment to Lily's thumping heart. Grace rocked in her chair and Carol fidgeted, even more uncomfortable now she was out of disguise. Harvey, the least likely of all of them to act, and yet, the one who did.

He sprang from his chair and, in a fluid motion, yanked the edge of the lace tablecloth from the cabinet, sweeping it off like an amateur magician. Such a small cloth. Ridiculous really, but when he threw it over Jamie, it was enough to confuse him as he swiped at it. Harvey grabbed the hardback chair from underneath Carol as she stood, or Rebecca, or whatever her name was now. He held the legs forwards to shepherd the butler into the corner of the room.

'Time for us to leave,' he called back, and the others didn't need to be asked twice. Elliot offered his hand to Lily. A fleeting moment of concern and care before they tumbled out of the room. Carol wobbled to her feet and offered

Grace a similar shelter, only to be batted away. Grace straightened her shoulders, her face fixed with pure determination.

Neither Elliot nor Harvey had bought them much time, just a few precious seconds, and that was all they needed to get out of the drawing room and into the hall. Harvey went last, edging backwards with the chair legs held high. As he passed through the door into the hall, Elliot was ready, and pushed it closed behind him. Then the two men wedged the back of the chair under the handle in the hope it would delay Jamie and the butler.

'Let's go to the attic,' Elliot said. 'I've got copies of all the keys up there and one of the old servants' rooms set up as a kind of control centre. There are cameras hooked up throughout the house and the feed goes straight to my laptop.'

Grace gave him a disapproving stare, but unless Lily was mistaken, her sparkle was coming back. 'Let's forget for a minute that you've been spying on us. You have keys, a computer and the Internet. That's it. That's our way out of here.'

Moving from one enclosed space to another with a madman on your heels struck Lily as a foolish thing to do. She'd seen enough horror films over the years. Her mind searched for an alternative, but on this occasion, it did seem the best option. They couldn't break out, so without a key they were trapped and at least this way they'd be together, they could close the hidden door behind them and the cameras meant they'd be able to keep tabs on what Jamie and the butler were up to while they waited for rescue.

The others didn't show any such concerns. Elliot pushed the wooden panel and lifted the tapestry to uncover the hidden entrance. The guests filed behind him, squeezing up the narrow staircase towards the servants' quarters. When they reached the landing on the first floor, Elliot took the opposite way to the one Lily had taken earlier.

Lily peeked at Harvey. He ascended backwards, using the back of his heel to feel for the next step, his body protecting the others in case anyone followed. The crashing sounds from the drawing room quietened the further up they climbed.

Lily knew a chair propped under a door handle wouldn't hold them inside for long. They'd simply rip the tape from the double doors and leave via the dining room. Their pursuers wouldn't be far behind.

The attic room Elliot so grandly called the 'control centre' was too small for five adults to fit into comfortably. Lily slipped into the space under the eaves, tucked up on the floor with her knees to her chest, her arms wrapped around them.

Elliot reached down to pull a laptop from underneath the chair. Not so in control now. Grace settled in the other chair. Carol stood awkwardly behind. There was no way Harvey was going to fit, so he became the unofficial doorway guard.

Flat screens mounted on the wall showed images of the house. The drawing room displayed on the middle and largest screen. Jamie and the butler were still in there. The lace cloth lay crumpled on the floor, surrounded by broken ornaments. They were inching the large cabinet away from the wall, edging it little by little, until they created enough space to manoeuvre behind it and retrieve the gun. The butler had removed his tailcoat. His face contorted as he slipped his arm into the gap.

Other screens showed the communal spaces. The dining room had been laid as if it were expecting guests to arrive, with places set and fresh candles waiting to be lit. No disturbance at all from Kevin's demise the night before. The conservatory, where the tables were bare, all lined up uniformly except for two chairs pulled out of place. Warm light bathed the majestic hallway, ready to welcome visitors. A smaller screen showed a rotating image of the working rooms. The office, the pantry and the kitchen.

'It's so we could coordinate mealtimes,' Elliot said. 'Make sure preparations were on track, that sort of thing. We needed to make sure guests weren't using a room we needed to set up.' It made sense. But something looked wrong.

Lily squinted at the image. 'Can you make it stay on the office, please? I think that's Debbie. It's too small to see. Is she okay?'

Elliot slid his fingertip across the pad and enlarged the image. Lily leaned forwards. She was right. It was Debbie. The once vivacious and frankly terrifying woman was now slumped across the desk. Like she'd fallen asleep working, except the angles were all wrong. They should get to her, find out if they could help her. None of them should be alone in the manor.

Elliot must have thought the same. 'I hate to sound callous, but checking on her will have to wait. There's nothing we can do for her now.'

Grace interrupted. 'All right, dear, enough of all this dallying. We need to get out of here. Being trapped in a small room where the only way out is a narrow staircase hasn't exactly improved our odds.' She pointed to the laptop. 'Will that thing connect to the Internet?'

Elliot tapped the keys. He hit them more and more vigorously, so clearly it wouldn't.

Lily unwrapped her arms from her knees. 'Whatever his reasons for wanting to kill us, Jamie set this whole thing up as a tribute to the great mysteries of all time, so we need to think like the famous detectives from the books we all love.' She implored Harvey. 'What would Mary Bakewell do?'

Harvey rubbed the side of his face. He took a deep breath before he spoke. 'In a novel, the detective would talk the killer down. They would regret their ways, make their confession, and leave peacefully with the police. I don't think any of us fancy trying to coax Jamie out of his plan, and there's no sign of the police.'

Grace slid from the chair and reached under the small coffee table in the corner. When she sat up, she held a long white cable covered in dust.

'Let's start by sorting out this laptop.' She reclaimed her chair and reached her other hand forwards to Elliot, showing she'd like him to pass her the laptop, which he did without a word. Grace fixed the Ethernet cable into the connection on the side and smoothed her fingers along the keys, familiarising herself with it.

She smiled at the shocked faces around her. 'Just because I was a housewife doesn't mean that's all I've ever done. I'm rather skilled at coding, so setting up an Internet connection shouldn't be too much of a challenge.'

Elliot tried unsuccessfully to hide his astonishment.

'I'll deal with this, dear. You find those keys.'

The image of Jamie and the butler in the drawing room shattered.

CHAPTER 43

J amie wanted his revenge, and he wanted that gun to help him get it. He'd waited so long and now, at last, he could take action. Their annoying escape routine had detracted from the plan, but he was confident his prey couldn't get out of the manor. Last night he'd sent Nicholas on a mission around the manor to make sure, while he'd been busy keeping Elliot occupied.

The two men eventually heaved the cabinet away from the wall. Nicholas rolled up his shirt sleeve and reached behind. Like a thin piece of fabric would make a difference.

When Jamie had resolved to find his biological parents all those years ago, he hadn't known what to expect, but a half-brother hadn't been on the list. Nicholas displayed the family trait of being easy to manipulate, just like Kevin.

He clenched his fist. 'Hurry up. I want the gun.'

Nicholas stretched, but his shoulder got in the way and hit the edge of the cupboard. He needed more space. Shoving the heavy cabinet out a bit more, he tried again.

Jamie sensed he was being watched. That wouldn't do. He grabbed a heavy ornament from the mantelpiece and launched it at the main camera in the room. He'd heard the parade stomp upstairs to the control room, and he didn't want an audience while they struggled to retrieve the gun. Clever Elliot wasn't so clever after all, leading them all up into a confined space. All Jamie needed to do was get the gun, bring them back downstairs like the naughty guests they were, and finish his game.

Daylight crept around the heavy curtains, sharing promises of a new day. One his guests would not be around to enjoy.

Nicholas lay flat on the floor, his chest pressed against the cabinet, his face reddened with the exertion.

Jamie gave the cabinet another shove and nudged Nicholas with his trainer. 'Get out of the way,' he said. 'Honestly, I have to do everything myself.'

Jamie considered the gap and judged it to be just wide enough. There were advantages to having long, lean limbs. He reached his arm behind, stretching until he touched the cold metal of the gun and eased it towards him. He was fond of the historic piece with the revolving cylinder and heavy weighted handle, and for some reason he'd acquired it long before he knew he'd need it. Must have been fate. Its weight felt like power.

Nicholas panted. A pitiful smile on his face, like a puppy waiting to be given a treat. Yes, he'd been a surprise for sure, but he'd ended up being more useful than Jamie had expected. He'd spent almost as long training Nicholas for the weekend as Elliot, and where Elliot needed elocution lessons, Nicholas needed to learn not to speak at all, to blend into the background and become invisible. The symmetry pleased Jamie.

Elliot hadn't really needed a different accent for the weekend to work. It didn't make any difference in the grand scheme of things. Jamie just enjoyed toying with him and he'd got so much pleasure watching him battle with the sounds, believing his mastery of them was integral to the whole venture, and gradually losing more of himself to Jamie's whims.

Nicholas was five years older than Jamie. That meant naughty Mummy had been putting it about well before she'd cast him aside. He dreamed about what it would be like to see her navigate his weekend, but she'd developed all sorts of problems she couldn't cope with and took her own life before the opportunity arose. She could have learned a lot from Mary Bakewell. At least she'd faced her disgrace and stuck by her son. Jamie emerged from behind the cabinet, gun in hand. Success. Without instruction to the contrary, Nicholas started pushing it back towards the wall.

'Leave it.' Jamie tried not to snap. This wasn't the time to tidy up. They had other priorities. Yes, Nicholas might well be another handy puppet, but he wasn't too bright.

'Come on,' he said.

Nicholas followed obediently, rolling his shirt sleeve back down. Jamie reached for the handle of the drawing room door and pushed. It was blocked and wouldn't open. He spun round and shoved Nicholas out of the way. He strode across to the double doors and ripped off the yellow tape. They made their way through the dining room and back out into the hall, where Jamie couldn't help but give a smirk at the chair balanced against the handle of the drawing room door. He kicked the chair out of the way. Whatever gave them the illusion of safety, he supposed. Now they were all in the attic, trapped. Jamie could easily pop up there and shoot them all. No, not quite all. After disposing of Max and the scuffle with Elliot, he only had four bullets left, so would need to choose wisely. Let someone watch the others die and then deal with them in another, more creative way. His plan covered that eventuality, too. He'd always thought that shooting the entire group would be far too dull.

First, he wanted them to know. To understand why he'd brought them all here and what their destiny was going to be as a consequence of their poor behaviour. He pressed his palm to the panel and the entrance to the servants' staircase popped open. Nicholas followed. No need to rush. They had all the time in the world. When they reached the landing, he left Nicholas guarding the junction.

'Stay,' he said. 'If you hear them coming down, shout for me.'

He was pretty sure Elliot would've led them straight up to the control centre, but the last thing he needed was to head up there, only to find they'd hidden in the storage room and doubled back once he'd passed. Jamie took the last few steps alone.

CHAPTER 44

Lily shuffled closer to Grace as she worked. She held the power button on the laptop; it beeped, and the screen flickered off.

'No need to act so surprised,' Grace said. 'Computers are my thing. My dear Arthur was the doer. I'm a thinker. Never was cut out to be a housewife. I'll tell you all about it when we get out of here. Ah, here we go.'

The laptop beeped again as it came back on.

'Incredible what you can do if you switch it off and back on again.' She moved across the keys with the dexterity of a digital native. 'Okay. I'm on the police website. There's only a place to report non-emergencies. I'll do that anyway.'

Grace squinted at the screen, talking the others through the steps she was taking. 'It says to call 999 for emergencies. How ridiculous. If we had access to a phone, we wouldn't be doing this. I'll try instant messaging and see how we get on. I've got a call app downloading in the background, so that should be ready when I'm done. Although it might take a while; this connection is pretty slow.'

Lily leaned forwards. 'We can message Steve, my housemate. He's practically glued to his phone.'

'Perfect,' Grace said. 'Let's start with him.'

Lily leaned over and tapped out a message. She'd never known Steve to be without his phone, so surely he'd pick up the message and send help. As long as he wasn't still asleep after a night out, or worse, he assumed she was winding him up. She prayed it wouldn't be too long.

The manor gave the impression of being isolated, but it wasn't. She and Max had walked from the centre of town on Friday without any bother and hopefully the storm hadn't caused too much disruption. It hadn't sounded that bad last night. She felt a flicker of optimism. Maybe it would be okay. Maybe they'd bought just enough time.

Heavy footsteps thudded up the narrow stairs, stamping on that hope. Harvey coughed and squeezed to the side, revealing Jamie. He pointed the revolver into the room.

Jamie caught sight of Grace with the laptop. 'Tut tut,' he said. 'Old ladies shouldn't play with technology. They might get hurt, and maybe shot.' Grace lowered the lid and clicked it closed.

'Time for you all to go back downstairs where I told you to be. We haven't finished the story yet and I'm sure you all want to keep going until the bitter end.'

No one moved.

'Now, please. Downstairs and take your seats for dinner.' He waved the gun.

Lily found the place setting with her name and took her seat. She didn't need to be told this time. None of them did. They'd seen the table set for dinner from the control room, fine crockery flanked by silver cutlery as if inviting them for a pleasant evening, even though it was still early morning. Jamie passed the butler a plastic lighter, and he circled the table, lighting candles that bathed the room in soft, flickering light.

They waited, subdued, in the six places that were left. Four for the guests, one for Elliot and one for Jamie, who stood behind the chair at the head of the table, the revolver in hand. No seat for the butler, who attended to his duties just like dinner was about to be served. He retrieved a bottle of red wine from the rack and wrapped the base with a white cloth. He leaned around them one by one, poured the wine and, when they each had a full glass, stood just behind Jamie.

Lily peeped at the others. Elliot sat to her side, no longer worthy of a place at the top of the table, no longer cast as lord of the manor. Elliot's head was bowed, his shoulders slumped. Jamie's eyes sparkled as he watched them take their seats. He could just shoot them all now, but it seemed he still wanted them to understand, as though it were as important as their demise. Lily expected Harvey to be the first to speak. He'd shown so much knowledge and skill this weekend. His actions had saved them from Jamie last time, but it was Carol, or rather Rebecca, who broke the silence. She had almost as many secrets as Jamie. Without the wig and the prosthetic nose, she could be a different person, the childminder Lily remembered so fondly.

Carol vocalised what they must all have been thinking. 'Why are you doing this?'

'Ah, you want the big reveal.' Jamie patted the edge of the table like he was testing out a piano key.

He addressed the butler. 'Should we oblige, do you think? Let them in on all the secrets before they pay the price for their atrocities.'

He was playing with them.

'Let's recap what we know so far.' He sneered at his classroom of captives. 'I was eight when I found out I'd been adopted. Quite a shock for a little boy, as you can imagine. The adults I loved and trusted as my parents no longer loved or trusted each other. In fact, my adoptive mother decided she would prefer to live with another man than with the man who I thought was my father.

'Single parents weren't common then, and single fathers were even less so. We muddled through. Him a little cold, me a little isolated. He treated me like a miniature adult. Expected the same standard of behaviour from me as any other grown-up. Except, as a child, I always failed. No room for emotion in our house. Real men don't show their emotions. A useful life lesson, I've found. After mother number two exited, we packed up the family home and moved to a smaller house, easier to maintain. Less fussy, more practical. People helped. One neighbour gave me dinner in the evenings, another came and cleaned once a week.'

He snarled at Carol. 'But we've covered that already.'

'That's when you came to my school,' Elliot said.

'Yes.' Jamie carried on with the part of the story he wanted to tell. 'But before all that, Kevin found out my brother wasn't his just after my mother left; I never knew how. I'd been too young to remember him, so you can imagine my surprise when I turned eighteen and accessed the records.'

He paused to let his words sink in, a frown on his face. 'Let me formally introduce you to Nicholas.'

The butler took a bow.

'My half-brother and partner for this event.'

Nicholas grinned and waved from the hip.

'I remember that,' Grace said. 'Arthur told me about a case where he discovered a man who'd abandoned two boys. He arrested him and brought him to justice. He found the boys and took them to safety.'

'We weren't abandoned. We were together.'

'No, that's not true, I'm afraid. It took them days to work out where you were. He'd abandoned you without food or heating. Arthur followed up on the case, told me they'd found the boys loving homes.'

Jamie disregarded her comments. 'He lied. We should never have been separated.'

He moved on to Elliot. 'Years I put up with you. Nervous little Elliot, so unsure of himself, so sure people wouldn't like him and his perfect life. But you were useful to keep around, I'll admit, and this whole thing was actually your idea. We sat for hours in a café in Italy talking about creating a real murder mystery, one that would bring together people who didn't know something connected them, and let them all be detectives.'

Elliot trembled, but his voice stayed strong. 'I never imagined real people would die. I imagined a fictional setup; why would I think any different? That's insane.'

'Now, now. There's no need to be critical. We're way past that. You were content to work out all the details from the celebrated novels and weave them into our house. Kept you out of the way while Nicholas and I decided on the guest list and invited everyone who deserves to be punished. I still can't believe you agreed to be the main host after the toss of a coin.'

'You rigged it?'

'Ah, the penny drops. Anyway, enough explaining for now. I think it's time for another game.'

Nicholas opened the cabinet and retrieved a pack of playing cards. He unwrapped the cellophane and slipped the deck from the packet. Nicholas counted out a card for each of them and fanned them face down. He offered Harvey the blue-backed selection first.

'No peeking,' Jamie said. 'You'll all get a card.' Harvey pinched the second from the end and placed it on the table in front of him without looking at it.

'Fancy that,' Nicholas said. 'The big man can follow instructions, after all.' He toured the table, delivering cards. Carol cupped hers in her hand; Lily cradled hers on her lap, trying to hide her shaking again.

When there was only a single card left, Nicholas rested it on the table in front of Elliot. 'One for the esteemed host.'

He was right, but Jamie was in charge, and he gave the instructions. 'We're going to turn our cards over one by one and whoever has the lowest card will be the next to die. Simple.'

Elliot got up from the table. 'This is madness. You can't make us do this. You can't just stand there and announce you're going to murder us all, as if you were deciding whose turn is next at a party game.'

Jamie waved the gun at him. 'Oh, but I can. And that is exactly what I intend to do.'

He looked directly at Elliot and held his stare until Elliot recoiled and sank back down, defeated.

'Lily, would you like to show your card first?' It was clearly a command, not a question.

Lily did as she was told, and her face froze.

'Show the room, if you will.'

She flipped the card to face the others. The ace of diamonds.

'For the purposes of the game, I think we'll say that aces are high.'

The others showed their cards as directed until they each had a number.

Carol had the lowest card, a four of clubs. She cried out. 'I'm so sorry, beautiful boy. I never wanted to hurt you. That's just the way things were, how we dealt with troubled children. There wasn't the support available then, to get you help. I wish with all my heart it could have been different.'

Her shoulders shook with terror as she faced her tormentors. She gripped the table for support and begged for her life. The others sat frozen, powerless.

Elliot reached for the full glass in front of him and flung it across the table as though it could knock the gun or distract Jamie, but all he achieved was a table covered in red wine. Carol clasped her hands and waited to die. Jamie held up the gun, pure, evil delight on his face. Lily squeezed her eyes closed and waited for the inevitable gunshot.

CHAPTER 45

An explosion. But not the gunshot she'd expected. Lily looked up as another crash came from the front of the house. Armed police bundled through the door in formation. They separated, chose positions around the room. Some crouched, others stood, all held guns focused directly at Jamie and Nicholas. The black-clad police, with heavy boots and padded vests, were so unlike the officer from the evening before, their appearance incongruous to the setting. They scanned the room, aware of the smallest movement, evaluating what was a threat.

Jamie's antique revolver suddenly looked ridiculous compared to the police weaponry. He lowered it cautiously and held it by his side. Not ready to give up control. Nicholas stood statue-like once more, like he could evade detection by staying in character. Lily raised her hands in surrender. Just in case.

A man strode in. He wore a suit under a bullet-proof vest. He held his palms in front of himself and addressed Jamie, ignoring the rest of the room.

'Son. Put the gun down.' He spoke like a man used to being listened to. Arthur used to do that.

Nicholas raised his hands. Jamie took a beat longer to respond, possibly debating whether he could do anything other than comply, whether it was worth removing one last guest from the equation before the police took him in. Lily crushed the card she still held on her lap. Elliot reached under the table and took hold of her hand. Jamie made his decision, settled the gun on the table and raised his hands above his head.

An armed police officer swooped in with a gloved hand to take the revolver away. With a practised motion, he made the gun safe, slipped it into a clear plastic bag, and departed, like it had never been there. Two others materialised behind Jamie and Nicholas, took their hands from above their heads and secured them behind their backs, before leading them away.

What happened next was a complete blur. The adrenaline of fear and hope for survival replaced by exhaustion and a willingness to submit completely to the instructions of professionals who would take care of them. Heavy boots thumped in the background as they made a search of the property. Grace's posture showed her defiance, her classic elegance shining through her grief. Carol cupped her face and sobbed.

Harvey reached out his hand to the suited officer.

'Detective Brown,' the officer said, shaking the offered hand.

Lily strained to hear something in the background. 'Shh.' She tilted her head, not caring if she was being disrespectful to the authorities. 'What's that? Can anyone else hear a murmur?'

She didn't wait for confirmation as she dashed through the double doors to the drawing room and dropped once more to Max's side, this time with hope. He made a soft groan, his eyelids flickered.

Lily picked up his hand once more and shouted. 'Help! Max is still alive.'

Behind her, Detective Brown echoed her request, making the ask more specific as he shouted for paramedics to enter. Kind hands moved Lily out of the way and she swayed, numb, with her arms wrapped around her waist while the paramedics did their work, stopped the bleeding and took vitals. They rolled Max onto a trolley and whisked him away. Elliot found his way to her side and gently, but firmly, pulled her away from the scene.

Detective Brown perched next to Grace. He draped a blanket around her, like Lily had earlier.

She pulled it tight. 'Thank you,' she said. 'You'll find my dear husband Arthur in our room. We knew he only had a few months left, so I doubt you'll find anything suspicious. Either way, I'd be grateful to know.'

'Is that what the pills were for?' Lily said, then remembering her manners, she continued, 'I saw them on the nightstand when we came up to you this morning. The same bottle I saw in Max's room.'

Detective Brown scratched a few words in his notebook. 'We'll look into it, thank you.'

'Please do,' Grace said. 'Arthur stopped taking medication a while back. He said it made him groggy, and he wanted to enjoy his last few weeks. He hated the constant fatigue his condition gave him and swore the vitamins helped take the edge off. At least his mind was sharp, just like the old days.'

'That's why he didn't come to afternoon tea,' Lily said.

'Yes, dear, he was getting worn out and needed a lie down. I'm so glad he solved one last case, even if it's ended up being more than we bargained for.'

Harvey poured coffee from a pot and gave her a cup.

'You've been through a lot, I can tell.' Detective Brown spoke in a soft, yet determined tone. 'I'm sure you all want to get home as quickly as possible, so I'll just take a few details and we'll arrange transport. We can deal with more formal statements over the next few days, as long as we get the main points down now.'

'Thank you, Detective,' Elliot said. 'I suppose I should start. I'll tell you what was supposed to happen and explain where it deviated so horribly from the script.'

'Before that, can you tell us if Debbie's okay?' Lily said. 'She's in the office by the kitchen. We saw her on the camera.'

'She's in the best possible hands. They'll take care of her.'

Not an answer as such, but more an implication that she might still be alive.

Detective Brown asked endless questions and wrote up statements. Eventually, they made their way out into the fresh morning air. An eery stillness settled on Kendrick Manor. Light clouds drifted across the sky. Max and Lily would not travel together this time. They'd rushed him and Debbie to the hospital. Lily decided she'd visit later.

A police officer opened a car door for her, and she climbed into the back. They journeyed up the gravel driveway and passed through the iron gate back out into the real world. She settled her head against the window, grateful to be going home. Suddenly, that magnolia room didn't seem so bad.

CHAPTER 46

Lily arranged another stack of books into a box, closed the flap and pressed brown tape over the seal.

Max wisely kept out of the way, sitting on the bare mattress, his back against the headboard and his arm in a sling. 'You weren't kidding when you said you've got a lot of books. Don't you ever throw any away?'

Lily put her hand to her heart and inhaled sharply. 'Certainly not. You can't throw books away.'

She lowered her hand, grinned, and tapped his shoes, slipping a piece of newspaper underneath so he wouldn't get the mattress dirty. Just because this wouldn't be her room anymore didn't mean she couldn't keep it tidy for the next person. He chuckled. She didn't mind. She took the marker pen from the floor, pulled off the lid with her teeth and wrote 'BOOKS' on the top.

'Maybe some of them could find their way to the library in the youth centre,' she said. 'Inspire the next generation of book lovers.'

'Great idea,' Max said. 'Sorry I can't be more help today.'

'I'm just glad you're here.'

She touched his good shoulder. He was under strict instructions from the hospital not to do any heavy lifting, but he had insisted on coming over for moral support as she packed, instead of waiting at the flat. She'd visited him every day while he'd been in hospital, brought him books and bunches of grapes. He admitted later he'd given the grapes away, not being a big fan of fruit. She supposed they'd learn lots of details like that about each other. Now they were going to share Theo's old flat. When he'd suggested she rent the spare room, she'd jumped at the chance.

Lily's mother had shrieked with joy when she discovered her spinster daughter planned to move in with a dashing young man. An artist, nonetheless, how Bohemian. Not that their relationship could ever be anything other than platonic. Lily decided not to tell her about Elliot, not for a while, anyway. It would spoil the surprise. She filled another box.

A car horn beeped from the street below. Lily pulled up the sash and leaned out of the window as a small grey van pulled up outside. Elliot emerged from the driver's side and, spotting Lily leaning out of the window, gave her a wave. In jeans and a blue plaid shirt, he couldn't look more different to the historic host he'd been at Kendrick Manor.

Lily gave him a wave and called down. 'It's open.'

He smiled up at her, rewarding her with that dimple she liked so much.

In the simple magnolia room, she'd stacked the boxes in a neat row. Elliot gave Lily a peck on the cheek and shook Max's free hand. Lily's phone pinged.

'It's Grace,' she said. 'She's wishing us luck with the move and inviting us round for a reunion dinner next weekend.'

'As long as she doesn't make prawns,' Max said. 'Remember Arthur's story about getting food poisoning?'

'Good point,' Elliot said. 'Hopefully no steak either. I don't think I'll ever eat that again.'

'Will Debbie be there, do you think?' asked Lily.

'I think so, yes,' Elliot said. 'I spoke to Milly, her old PA, and she's taking a sabbatical. The head injury needed surgery, but she's recovering well and thinking about setting up her own business. I'm sure we'll hear all about it. I can't imagine Debbie not working.'

'We never found out what grudge Jamie had against her.' Max shifted his feet on the bed, and Elliot perched on the edge.

'I spoke to Detective Brown yesterday.' Lily leaned down to tape up another box. 'He couldn't give all the details while they're building the case, but apparently Jamie tried to steal money from Debbie's company a few years back. She found out about the scheme and stopped him. He was never charged, but he wanted revenge.'

'That must have been before my parents invested. He said he'd tried to get funding for the manor before we asked them. I thought he meant a bank loan.'

'Like you would,' said Max. 'Any insight into why he chose the rest of us?'

'Well, the childhood home he mentioned was repossessed and auctioned after his father ran off. It's the same building Theo converted into the youth centre. Jamie resented anything even remotely related to his lost childhood. Theo wasn't an option, so he transferred the blame to you.'

'Kind of him. And what about Harvey?'

'Pure jealousy. Jamie followed Mary Bakewell's career and couldn't help comparing Harvey's life to his own. He couldn't reconcile his own rejection with the love Mary gave Harvey and formed quite the obsession.'

'It's Nicholas I feel sorry for,' Elliot said. 'Sounds like he was living a pretty normal life until Jamie came along and manipulated him.'

'Jamie did have a natural charm,' Lily said. 'He fooled us all.'

Elliot bent and lifted the first box. He winced. 'What's in this thing?'

'They're all full of books.' Max laughed.

''Course they are. Better take them one at a time.' Elliot carried the first out through the house to load into the back of the van.

Max flinched as he swung his legs off the bed, leaving a torn piece of newspaper behind. 'I'll let you say goodbye to the room.'

He ignored her protests and lifted a black sack of clothes over his good shoulder. He gave a brief nod to Lily's soon-to-be ex-housemate on the landing. Steve brushed his blonde hair out of his eyes and leaned against the door frame. He held his phone.

'Hey, Lils,' he said. 'You wanna to tell me where you're heading, just in case you get caught up with another serial killer?'

Lily reached out her arm and pulled him into a hug. 'I should be okay this time. I still don't know what would have happened if you hadn't seen the message we sent and told the police about the manor.' She pulled back and squeezed his arm. 'Thank you.'

'No worries,' he said. 'You've got my number if you ever need me. Pub on Friday, if you fancy it?'

'I'll see you there.'

His phone rang, and he held it up. 'Got to take this. Good luck. We'll catch up Friday.'

He walked away, leaving her alone.

Lily gazed around the nearly empty room. The stripped bed, the empty wardrobe, the desk and chair. She'd leave the desk. Max had said she could use an old writing bureau of Theo's and she'd told him she'd be honoured. Her last task was to remove the plot web she'd fixed to the wall. She peeled away the multicoloured ribbons, folded them carefully and placed them in a shoe box. The photos came last, pictures cut from magazines, photos printed from the Internet. It was how she plotted, how she crafted her stories. These were her characters, the businesswoman, the country gent, the jabbering man, the ex-detective and his wife, the disagreeable man, the woman with all the secrets. All linked back to a murderer and his brother, the butler. Jamie was safely in custody, and despite everything, he'd given her the gift of the perfect plot. She couldn't wait to write up the story.

FREE SHORT STORY

Curious to know what Lily wrote after she escaped Kendrick Manor?
To download your exclusive free short story go to www.jodyderby.com/8pm
Enjoy!

ABOUT JODY DERBY

Jody Derby loves a good murder. Fictional ones, just so we're clear. Preferably where the gore level is low, and the humour sprinkled liberally like mystery glitter.

She writes contemporary murder mysteries and thoroughly enjoys thinking up creative ways to do away with her characters.

As a Londoner, she's good at walking quickly through crowded places and avoiding eye contact with people on public transport.

Jody's an aspiring yogi, jogger and strength trainer, all of which she does a bit, but should probably do more of because she sits down quite a lot and is rather partial to cake.

www.jodyberby.com

Enjoyed this book?

You can make a difference. Reviews help bring a book to the attention of other readers.

If you enjoyed this book, I'd be grateful if you can spare a few minutes to leave a review wherever you purchased it.

Thank you so much

Jody

ACKNOWLEDGMENTS

I've wanted to write a novel for as long as I can remember and it turns out it's a massive learning curve. Along the way, I've met some wonderful authors at all different stages of their careers, who have motivated and inspired me, often without knowing it.

Of course, there's a bit more to publishing than simply writing a story, and I've been lucky enough to work with some incredibly talented people along the way. Thank you to Hannah McCall at Black Cat Editorial for all your advice and encouragement, and to Tania at MiblArt for making the cover design process so straight forward.

Thank you to Sacha Black and the Rebel Author community who helped push me over the line to actually get the book done. You are all so welcoming and supportive; I truly feel that I've found my tribe.

To Mum for taking me to the library when I was little and for always encouraging my love of reading.

And last, but no means least, thank you to you, the reader; for reading all the way to the end. It means the world.

Printed in Great Britain
by Amazon